THE REIGN OF THE DRAGON

BOOKS IN CHURCH OF THE SEER

The Dark Reveal

CHURCH OF THE SEER

THE REIGN OF THE DRAGON

KENYA FOUCH

BOOKLOGIX
Alpharetta, Georgia

ISBN: 978-1-6653-0723-9 - Paperback
eISBN: 978-1-6653-0724-6 - eBook

Library of Congress Control Number: 2023923205

☉This paper meets the requirements of ANSI/NISO Z39.48-1992 (Permanence of Paper)

1 2 2 0 2 3

For my dad.

CHURCH OF THE
SEER

① 1

WELCOME BACK

Charles Connaught sat at his desk in the private office at the rear of the Connaught Hotel headquarters in Islington with his face in his hands, in disbelief. A large portrait of his wife, Bailey, was positioned above the mantle in the office. Bailey passed away two years prior, and Charles was grateful that she would never know the pain that was currently tormenting his spirit. The news, delivered by MI6, that their son Jackson was killed during what had been described as a supernatural weather occurrence at the Vatican had taken its toll on him. Charles hadn't slept or eaten since he received the news, and his support staff began to worry about his quickly fading complexion. Jackson was the sole heir to the Connaught fortune and had recently announced his candidacy for president in the 2048 election. Charles just couldn't accept that a light so bright could so quickly and easily be extinguished, especially without someone to hold accountable. To make matters worse—or at least more complicated—the rumor mill was buzzing with the news that

Jackson's wife, Kiera, delivered a son in Italy that was fathered by Jackson's childhood rival, Ukweli Aseyori. In addition to Jackson, the storm was also thought to be the cause of death for the head of the Church of the Seer, Remington Cross.

Charles questioned MI6 concerning the likelihood of two prominent heads of combatant organizations dying under such mysterious circumstances, but neither the British government, the American government, nor reps from the Company offered any information to calm his growing frustrations. Charles wanted answers and he knew where he could get them. He put in a standing request to Drs. Kobe and Mara Aseyori, Ukweli's parents and beneficiaries of the generosity of the Connaught family charities, that he be notified immediately upon the return of Ukweli, and Kiera, to Atlanta.

Charles arranged for Jackson's body to be flown from Italy to London and he went to the airport to meet the plane with three men from a local mortuary. He watched from the passenger seat of the company SUV as the cargo plane maneuvered on the tarmac and into position. It was a feeling that no parent should ever have to experience. It was out of the natural order of things. Parents shouldn't have to bury their children.

As the plane came to a stop, tears began to flood Charles's eyes so that he could barely see the rear door of the plane open. He stepped outside of the vehicle and prepared his soul for what would undoubtedly be the unforgettable image of men carrying the coffin containing the body of his only son. He wiped his eyes and squinted as seven men exited the rear of the plane. He blinked several times. He wiped his eyes and squinted again. His face flushed pale and his jaw dropped so low, he wasn't sure he could ever close his mouth again. Right in the middle of the group of men exiting the plane was his son, alive. Charles simultaneously experienced elation and terror.

"Jackson? Jackson! Is it really you? How is this possible?" He stumbled over toward Jackson and put his hands on his face. The tears began to flow again.

"It's okay, Dad. I'm okay. I'm sorry for scaring you."

"Scaring me? They told me you were dead!"

"Well, I was. But I'm back."

"This is a miracle! But, how?"

"I'll explain everything, but for now, let's get something to eat. I'm starving."

(**2**)

FOR UNTO US

U kweli sat with Kobe, Mara, Adam, and Paul in the waiting room at Ospedale di Santo Spirito in Sassia, just east of Vatican City. Kiera had gone into labor following the unexplained meteorological phenomenon at the Vatican and was set to deliver any minute. The doctors usually invite the father into the delivery room, but the stress of long-distance travel coupled with her antenatal history created risks for Kiera the doctors decided would be better addressed without distractions. There was no time for an epidural, so the delivery was very painful, and Kiera lost a lot of blood. There were concerns of hypovolemic shock and the doctors weren't entirely sure whether Kiera would pull through due to the sheer amount of trauma and stress on her system.

The waiting was hard. Ukweli sat in a stiff wooden chair and wondered how things could've changed so quickly. It was only a few short days ago that he was Captain Ukweli Aseyori, leader of the fiercest strike team in the Church of the Seer, building a life in Atlanta with Ava. Now, he sat in a hospital in Rome, waiting for his childhood sweetheart to give birth to their son, who'd been conceived in adultery.

On top of that, the Church of the Seer now only existed in theory. Remington Cross was dead—in fact, he had been dead for quite some time. Actually, he rationalized, the Church of the Seer never really existed, at least not as it was presented to him. He had given up his career as a star on the pitch to pursue justice for the murder of his sister, and now it was all over. It was all a sham. He hadn't made the difference he thought he was making.

His marriage was probably over. His relationship with Ava mostly seemed like a business arrangement anyway. They had gotten closer, he thought, but he wondered if all the drama of the past few days even meant anything to her. She was loyal to the Church first and foremost. With the collapse of the Church and the death of Cross, he wondered if she would leave. Did he even want her to stay?

Ava was an experienced nurse and surprisingly offered aid to the understaffed emergency room unit, given Kiera's complicated delivery. The irony was not lost on Ukweli. When the process was completed, Ava updated Ukweli on the condition of the baby and mother.

"Ava, give me some good news, please."

"Ukweli, your baby is fine."

"And Kiera?"

"Kiera will be fine eventually. She's out of the woods, in so much as her life isn't in danger at this point, but she's been through a lot. The doctors were amazing in there, they literally saved her life."

"I understand. I'm grateful for them. I really owe you too."

Ava grabbed Ukweli by the arm at the elbow and led him around the corner to a small breakroom. The pleasant aroma of freshly ground coffee and warm cinnamon buns provided a strong aesthetic contradiction to Ava's grim countenance.

"Ukweli, we need to talk."

"We do. We will."

"UK, we need to talk *now*."

"You want to do this right here?" Ukweli made a gesture that suggested he was embarrassed to have such a sensitive conversation in front of so many people—even though there was no one else in the room.

"Look, I just helped deliver your baby. I told you how that girl felt about you, and time and again you insisted that it wasn't a big deal. You lied to me. Then you slept with her, in our bed no less. And then you lied to me again. Please tell me how I'll ever be able to trust you?"

"Trust me? Ava, everything you said is true. I should've confronted my feelings for Kiera long before she came over that night. I can admit that. But listen, I'm not going to simply overlook the fact that you held a gun to my father's back. I know that our marriage was nothing more than an occupational responsibility for you." Ukweli realized he was making a gun with his hand and pointing it at Ava's temple. He relaxed his arms and tried to take a less intimidating posture.

"You're such a damn fool, UK. I love you! I got on that plane with Kelley and Cross to make sure your parents were safe. I played along until I couldn't anymore. Honestly, I'm still not sure what happened in the end. Regardless, I've always been here for you. You've done nothing but deceive me. But even after all that, here I am, trying to make sure you and your son and your concubine are okay. God! When will I learn?!" Ava threw up her hands and started to walk away.

"Look, Ava, I know we have some challenges—"

Ava quickly turned to face Ukweli. "Challenges?! Have you gone insane? Do you think I didn't see your face when Jackson grabbed Kiera's hair and forced her to her knees? You were ready to walk through fire for her! And that was before you knew the baby was yours! I know you love her, and she obviously loves you too. And now, the baby . . . honestly, I don't even know why I'm here."

"Just because I have feelings for Kiera doesn't mean that I don't love you." Ukweli gently reached for Ava's hand, but she aggressively moved away.

"Boy, stop. You love that girl and now y'all have a kid together. Do you really think I'm gonna stick around and watch the two of you coparent while you try to pretend she's not in love with you?" Ava turned her back to Ukweli and sighed. Ukweli walked up behind her and put his hands on her shoulders.

"Listen, I know a lot of things have changed in a very short time. I'm sorry for the role I played in the pain and confusion you're feeling now. But can you please just give me time to process all of this before you make any rash decisions?"

Ava turned to face Ukweli. "UK, I love you. I really do. But there's no way this situation ends with you and me together and Kiera and your son on the outside looking in. There's no way I'll ever be a priority in your life again."

"Hey, let's take some time to let the changes soak in. We'll sit down and really discuss things when we get back to Atlanta. We need to get some rest so we can organize our new lives with clear minds. Can you just give me that?"

One of the doctors emerged from the restricted area and slowly peeked into the breakroom. He timidly came over to Ukweli. "The patient is stable and alert. She's in a great deal of pain but she should make a full recovery. She has asked to see you."

Ukweli returned his attention to Ava. "Babe, we'll talk about all of this when we get back to Atlanta. I promise."

"Babe." She scoffed sarcastically, rolled her eyes, and waved him off. "Just go."

Ukweli followed the doctor around a corridor and down two long halls before they arrived at the intensive care section of the labor and delivery wing. He took soft steps as he entered the room. Walking past the curtain, he saw Kiera lying in the bed and his eyes began to water. She had been through so much trauma, he could barely recognize her. Her face and body were swollen and pale. She looked like she had been to actual hell. He took the time to clear his face before he approached her.

"Do you still think I'm pretty?" She chuckled through a cough and winced in pain.

"You're more beautiful today than you've ever been."

"Ukweli, I'm so sorry."

"No, you don't have anything to apologize for."

"Yes . . . I really do. I started all this. I'm sorry for throwing myself at you that first night. I'm sorry I didn't tell you about the baby. I'm sorry—"

"Seriously, stop apologizing. You just need to rest."

"I realize that my decisions have turned your life upside down. That was never my intention."

"I'm sure you mean *our* decisions. You didn't do any of this alone."

"Look where it's gotten us though."

"Maybe it's for the best. I always felt guilty about moving in the shadows."

"Jackson was devastated when my first pregnancy failed, but he and I hadn't been together for months this time, so he knew this baby wasn't his. I had no right to put him through all of this."

"Kiera, we've all used questionable judgment and we've obviously done some things we aren't proud of. We can sort everything out later though, after you've rested. You've been through a lot."

"Oh, believe me, I know. I feel like I fell off a building."

"You did good though. Yoddah is perfectly healthy."

"You have absolutely lost your mind if you think I'm naming my child after some swamp frog."

Ukweli stepped back and put his hand over his mouth, showing genuine offense. "First of all, put some respect on Master Yoda's name. Besides, he was only on Dagobah because of the Empire . . . never mind. But not *Y-o-d-a*. *Y-o-d-d-a-h*. It means warrior in Hindi. I thought it would be a cool way to honor your mom."

"No, it's not."

"All I'm saying is—"

"Ukweli. No. Let it go." Even in pain, she managed to shake her head vigorously. She was still very bossy.

Virtus Pax Aseyori was born on October 21, 2044, in Rome. Ukweli didn't seem to notice Kobe, Mara, Ava, or Kiera as he walked out of the hospital and loaded the airport shuttle. He was beaming with pride, but he struggled with the concept that he was actually a father. Adam and Paul helped Kobe and Mara into the van and Ava assisted Kiera.

Everyone slept most of the flight back to Atlanta—except Ukweli. He couldn't stop staring at Pax. He had never known a love like this. He didn't even know it was possible. He gazed at him. He sang to him. He smelled him. He hugged him. Even when Ukweli's body demanded sleep, he only allowed himself to doze off for a few minutes at a time.

Ukweli did set aside time to speak with Alexander, who had returned to Atlanta with Charlotte and Kei to help process the bodies of Marcus and Calvin. Ukweli realized he had a lot of unfinished business and some tough conversations waiting for him on the ground. He decided to just enjoy the flight with Pax and that he would deal with the other stuff in time.

Thysia, please show me how to protect Pax. Teach me how to be a father.

Kiera woke up in the large bed in the room at the rear of the plane with Ava sitting on a small stool right beside her pillow. She was still in a lot of pain, but the sleep helped her stay cautious and alert dealing with Ava.

"Hey, how do you feel?" Ava's expression made Kiera uncomfortable.

"I was really out, huh?"

"Yeah, you definitely needed rest. We all did. Honestly, you need a lot more. Your body has been through it."

"Trust me, I feel it." Kiera paused for a moment. "Hey, can I ask you a question?"

"You mean, why am I helping you? Given that you're sleeping with my husband?"

"Well, that lacks context, but yes."

"Look, Jackson died in a way that I can't even explain, and then you almost died giving birth to a baby conceived in scandal. Right now, you probably feel ashamed and alone. At least, you should. I understand that feeling and I took an oath to never do harm."

"Hey . . . Ava . . . look, me and Ukweli—"

"Kiera, you don't have to explain it. And please don't

convince yourself that you need to lie. I know that you're in love with Ukweli. You've loved him for a long time. I get it. But guess what? He's my husband, and I'm not going anywhere. You're now the mother of his first child, so I guess you're not going anywhere either. But while you're responsible for Pax, I'm still responsible for Ukweli. When we get off this plane, he has to bury two of his squad members, figure out what to do with Kelley, pull together what's left of the Church of the Seer, and, somehow, learn how to be a dad. Not to mention the fact that he's now the Company's number one target. The last thing he needs is to deal with the two of us bickering. The last thing *you* need is any additional stress on your body. So, here's my suggestion. Be Pax's mom. Learn your role. Play your role. We'll figure it out as we go. You think you can do that?"

Kiera tightened her posture and tilted her head to the side. "Oh, I see. You want me to fade quietly into obscurity while you fix your relationship. Ukweli deserves to have real love in his life. Not some employee punching a time clock. Are you with him out of love or allegiance?"

"Honestly, Mrs. Connaught, I don't separate the two. And you're not in a position to question my motives while you wallow in the sludge of an ongoing affair like a pretty pink piggy. Plus, if push comes to shove, I'm an agent of the Church and you're a soccer player. I'll take great pleasure in beating your ass."

"Touché." Kiera bowed out while maintaining a coy smile of satisfaction knowing that Pax was here and no degree of ass-beating would ever change that.

3

THE NEW REALITY

OCTOBER 25, 2044

U kweli stood in the soggy grass at the burial plot in Westview Cemetery, just west of downtown Atlanta. His large, black umbrella struggled to protect him from the pouring rain and strong winds that added gloom to the already melancholy morning. He stood in front of two coffins, each containing the body of a member of his unit. Marcus and Calvin were elite soldiers who fought for the Church of the Seer, but both men were executed because of their allegiance to him. Ukweli knew that leaders accept responsibility, but he found this to be an unbearable weight. Ava stood beside him, under the same umbrella, equally unprotected from the elements. Adam and Paul stood behind him. Charlotte and Kei stood on the other side of the coffins with Alexander standing in between the two plots. Ukweli's voice quivered initially, but he grew strength from his team, regained his resolve, and spoke.

"Loyalty challenges us. It calls out the very best in us. What exactly do we stand for? Calvin and Marcus were two of the finest soldiers in the world. They were our friends. They were good men. They deserved better than this. I will be forever grateful for their sacrifice. I don't know exactly where we will go from here, but we owe it to these great men to figure it out, and together we will. They completed their mission. They have earned their rest. It's done."

OCTOBER 27, 2044

Kiera's parents flew in from New Delhi to care for her and Pax. Against Ukweli's wishes, they returned to her house in Decatur. Kiera still had to come to grips with the fact that her husband was dead. Jackson was mayor and a leading presidential candidate when he died, so she was grateful that their attorneys had already created a plan in the event of an untimely death. The city of Atlanta simultaneously mourned the loss of their beloved leader and gossiped about the allegations that the mayor's wife had been unfaithful. Kiera stayed in the house, mostly because her body needed to recover, but there was a part of her that was ashamed of what she had done. She didn't want to face the scrutiny and judgment the world had to offer. She hoped the news of Jackson's death would eventually move off the front page and she could return to a sense of normalcy—if there was such a thing anymore.

4

THE DRAGON CLAUSE

OCTOBER 24, 2044

Kobe and Mara got off the plane in London, only instead of their usual car and driver, they were met by a black sprinter van. The door opened and Charles Connaught got out.

"Welcome back, you two. I hope you enjoyed your vacation."

Charles helped Mara into the van before stepping to the side to clear a path for Kobe. The couple sat and was greeted by Ann Jefferson.

"Hi, guys."

"Ann." Kobe was noticeably agitated.

"Listen, about that business in Italy. I apologize for keeping you in the dark."

"And what of using us as pawns against our son?"

"We needed to know exactly how radical that speech was going to be. Of course, we didn't know that Thysia would intervene personally. That changed the stakes."

Mara spoke up. "You've been threatened by Ukweli since he was a boy. How much higher could the stakes be?"

"We knew about Ukweli, but we felt we could manage the threat as long as we had the two of you. But when Thysia showed up, that let us know it's bigger than Ukweli."

"Bigger than Ukweli? What do you mean?"

"The girl is his light. As long as we kept the two of them apart, the threat was minimal. The time for that has passed though. We were unsuccessful. Now we're at war with a new enemy."

"New enemy?"

"The child could destroy us."

"Pax?"

"If the child is allowed to mature and develop properly, he could become a weapon with immeasurable power. We simply cannot allow it. In fact, Thysia's involvement has prompted Jennifer's mobilization of the Dragon Clause."

Kobe looked confused. "Who is Jennifer? What is the Dragon Clause?"

Ann smiled, but not in a comforting way. It reminded Kobe of the way the Grinch smiled when he decided to steal Christmas. It made him uneasy and prompted him to sit up straight in his seat.

"I have complete authority here on Earth. Jennifer is the Company's authority in this galaxy. You could say she's my boss, but we're more like sisters. She's coming here, personally, to implement the Dragon Clause. In fact, she's already chosen and empowered her DayStar."

"Ann, I know that you don't expect Kobe or me to help you harm our son or our grandson in any way. I don't know who or what you think he is, but don't you dare tell me the Company has plans to go to war with Pax—a newborn baby."

"The two of you will continue at the university. We'll

need a security system upgrade for the case housing the machine. Don't worry about Ukweli or Pax. It won't matter anyway. There's nothing you can do to stop the Dragon's Reign."

Ukweli tossed as he slept. There was no peace in his rest, and he couldn't shake the feeling that he and his family were in imminent danger. He began to dream of Uzuri, his bare feet in that pool of blood at the bottom of the stairs in Lagos. He saw the faces of the torqs from the Underground and he heard the whistling hiss as the symbionts dissolved. Suddenly, the shadows began to close in around him until he was overtaken by darkness. He tried to scream but he couldn't make a sound. His limbs were frozen. He couldn't move. As he was bound in the darkness, there was a great flash of light in the sky and dense, red clouds began to spiral downward as a large red dragon fell from heaven and landed awkwardly, crashing in front of him. The dragon quickly recovered and advanced toward him. Ukweli looked down at a sleeping Pax, lying at his feet. The dragon moved with curved motions like a snake. The dragon opened its mouth and behind sharp, bloody teeth and a slithering forked tongue, green and gold gases began to ignite, forming a bolide in the dragon's throat. Just before the dragon devoured Pax, Ukweli woke up in a sweat and Ava jolted awake, immediately trying to comfort him.

"Hey, hey, it was just a nightmare. UK, it was a nightmare."

"It was so real. I couldn't move. The darkness had me bound and the dragon had Pax—"

"Ukweli, Pax is fine. It's the middle of the night, but we can call Kiera if you want to be sure."

"No, I don't want to wake them if they're sleeping. I probably just need some air." Ukweli got out of bed.

"Where are you going?"

"I don't know. Potato House Grill, I guess."

"Okay. Bring me back some hash browns. You know how I like them."

Ukweli sat at the counter in the Potato House Grill on Andrew Young. He enjoyed the feeling of the robust brew traveling down toward his stomach. There was something very soothing about a warm beverage. He placed the order for Ava's Denver scramble hash browns. He couldn't understand how she could eat that stuff and still look the way she did. *Good genes,* he assumed. He tried thinking of his upcoming meeting with Kelley. He had no idea what he would say to her when they finally met face-to-face again. She was very dangerous, and he was a little nervous. A patron walked in and sat next to him at the counter. He looked to his right and did a double-take.

"Hello, Ukweli."

Ukweli's eyes went wide. "Hope?"

"No, I get that a lot. Hope is my sister. My name is Unity." Unity had black hair with a shimmering lotus flower just behind her left ear. She wore a purple and silver dress at calf length with black combat boots. Unity looked exactly like Hope and the only difference Ukweli could immediately notice was a small tattoo of a thunderbolt on Unity's neck and that her voice was deeper.

"We've never met. How do you know me? How did you find me?"

"It's my job to know how to find you." She sipped from Ukweli's cup with her left hand and held a pistol in her right.

"You're here for a reason. I'm in danger, huh?"

"Yes."

"Am I in danger metaphorically, or literally right now?" Ukweli looked around as he spoke.

"Thirty seconds."

"I don't have any gear."

"Good thing you can fight then."

"How many?"

"Six."

"All rogue torqs?"

"All torqs. No rogues. It's a Company hit. They have a quiet bounty on your head."

"Quiet bounty?"

"No public, daytime attempts."

"Damn, I walked right into this one. Did you come to warn me or help me?"

Unity loaded a clip into the pistol. "Both."

Ukweli and Unity stood up and jumped over the counter to take shelter. They warned the staff to stay low. Gunfire rained in through the windows from outside in the parking lot. Ukweli grabbed a knife and a small frying pan. As the gunfire subsided, Ukweli stood up and threw the knife, striking the forehead of one of the assailants. The familiar hiss. Unity lunged from her crouched position and returned fire with a semiautomatic weapon, striking down three of the men. Ukweli jumped over the counter and surged through the shattered glass and rolled onto the asphalt parking lot. He dodged a punch from a large man and bent his knees. Ukweli swiftly swept his feet and punched down, through the man's ribcage, as he crashed into the ground.

He stepped to the next man and punched him in the gut, then the throat, and grabbed his face, quickly twisting until it popped. Again, the screeching hiss.

Ukweli calmly walked back inside, through the door, grabbed his to-go bag, dropped a ten-dollar bill, and got on his black, electric cycle. Unity walked over to him. He addressed her, impressed.

"Does Hope fight like you?"

"No."

"Thank you for your help."

"You'll need to be very careful. Don't go anywhere alone at night."

"I'll try."

"You need to assemble your team tomorrow morning. The Company is making a big announcement at ten a.m. You'll need to be prepared to respond."

"What kind of announcement?"

"It will change everything. You will want Pax with you as well."

"What does any of this have to do with Pax?"

"It has everything to do with Pax." Unity disappeared into the night.

⑤

KELLEY JACK

Ukweli walked into the Georgia Bureau of Investigation building on Panthersville Road in Decatur at six a.m. with Charlotte and Kei on either side. He had been dreading this meeting with Kelley Jack and, even this morning as he walked into the facility, he was still unsure as to what he would actually say to her. His encounters with Kelley in the past had proven to him she was relentless. She was cunning. She was lethal. He had seen her do things that pushed his understanding of duty and ethics, and he absolutely did not trust her. It was only because of his undeniable encounter with Thysia at the Vatican that he knew he had to face her.

Four agents escorted Ukweli, Charlotte, and Kei to a holding room where Kelley sat at a table in a bright orange jumpsuit. Her hands and feet were in cuffs attached to the table with small chains. Ukweli was absolutely amazed at how beautiful she was even as an inmate. He sat in a chair across the table from Kelley, as Charlotte and Kei stood behind him. Kelley's face was frozen. There was no emotion.

She just looked straight ahead. Ukweli felt like she was somehow staring *into* him, and it initially made him shift in his chair.

"Relax, UK. It's good to see you." She smiled and it helped Ukweli regain form.

"Really, is it?"

"Seriously, lockup isn't the place for me, even in a resort like this. If you hadn't come this morning, you would've had to find me in the streets later."

"You knew I was coming?"

"I was counting on it."

"You remember what happened in Rome?"

"I remember enough."

"Did he talk to you?"

"No. He showed me."

"He showed you what?"

"I couldn't hear, and I couldn't move, but I could see. He showed me what I was supposed to do."

"What are you supposed to do?"

"We're wasting time, UK. Get me out of here and let's go. You know what's coming so you know we have to hurry."

"Actually, I don't know."

"Yes, you do. He showed you too. In your dream."

"What dream?"

"Last night. You know the dragon is coming. You know Pax is in danger."

"How do you know about the dragon? How do you know about Pax?"

"You're not the only one who dreams, UK. We can talk at the office. Let's go! Kei, your hair looks awesome."

Kei blushed. She had recently gotten her long hair cut into a concave bob. Neither Ukweli nor Charlotte mentioned it.

Ukweli signed for Kelley Jack's unconditional release into his custody. He knew it meant absolutely nothing. If she wanted to disappear, she would.

6

JENNIFER DEVORE

Alexander Scott walked into the executive office of the Church of the Seer at 9:30 a.m. and was greeted by Hope. The entire team was there, seated around the conference table; Adam, Paul, Charlotte, and Kei, along with Ava, Kiera and her parents, Pax, being held by Kiera's mother, Kelley, and Ukweli. Hope and Alexander took their seats at the table and Ukweli stood up to address the room.

"Thank you all for coming on such short notice. I know that the past couple of weeks have brought some dramatic changes in our lives. We've experienced some things that, quite honestly, can be hard to believe and difficult to accept. I know that our loyalty has been tested. I know we mourn the loss of our friends. I know that, given what we now know of the Church of the Seer, you all may feel like you've been living a lie. Let today be proof that your efforts have not been in vain. We're assembled here this morning as the remnant of a movement with a dubious beginning. But we're going to take this organization and plant it on a rock. We're going to uphold the standards of the Church of the Seer and live out the creed that once only existed on paper. We're going to walk the walk. Ann Jefferson and the Company are making an announcement shortly. I don't know what they're going to do or say, but I know there is something coming that puts us all in jeopardy. Remember this, whatever it is, whatever they say, whatever their plan, we will face it together. Prepare your souls for anything and know that we *will* respond. I believe in you. Let's stick together and believe in each other!"

The television screens, laptops, and cell phones all powered on to reveal a waving white flag with a red dragon, the new seal of the Company.

The dragon from my dream, Ukweli thought to himself. The Company was known for dramatic reveals but this was different. There was no music or fanfare. This was ominous and dark. Everyone in the room felt it as they stayed silent.

"Just how in the hell are they continuously able to hack every device on the planet?" Ukweli said with genuine concern.

The flag faded to a black screen and a woman appeared. Her skin was perfectly tanned, as if she had just come in from sunning at the beach. Her hair was black with a few streaks of gray. It was not Ann Jefferson.

"Good morning citizens of Earth. I am Jennifer Devore, CEO of Imperium Intergalactic. We are the parent organization of what you have come to know as the Company. We are very proud of the progress you have made here in such a short period of time, and we're excited about our continued partnership as we progress in our quest to improve on God's good work."

Ukweli sat up in his chair. "This can't be good."

Jennifer continued. "We are instituting some major changes for the future of your planet, and I wanted to come personally to see to it that you're receiving the finest service in the galaxy. You'll be very excited to know that we are eliminating the ban on your holy books, and we have already begun mass distribution in key areas. Feel free to return to your religious services as you were before the expurgation. We, at Imperium Intergalactic, want to stress that you are our most valuable resource, and nothing is more important to us than your freedom. We will continue to use the HealthShare system to manage your well-being and as a system of distribution of resources. Remember, we have unlimited food and water at our disposal so there is no need for any citizen of this planet to go without. Of course, we also value your freedom; should you so choose, you can forgo the HealthShare chip and go out in search of resources for yourself and your family on your own. Please remember that in order to access any and all Imperium Intergalactic resources, you must enroll in the HealthShare network and receive the chip. Now, I've saved the very best news for last. We searched the ends of the earth, and even local systems, for the very best person to lead our new initiatives on your planet. As fate would have it, that person has been here all along. Please help us honor and reintroduce, the new DayStar of the Company and the very handsome face of the franchise, Jackson Connaught!"

Kiera stood up. "That … that's impossible." Her whispered words accurately conveyed her disbelief, but her face could not hide her fear and shame. Her hands began to shake and her already soft voice cracked. "It has to be some sort of hologram or a camera trick."

The rest of the room watched in stunned silence as Jackson Connaught stood and prepared to speak. Ava closely watched Ukweli to gauge his reaction, which reflected his curiosity and confusion.

"My fellow citizens, what a glorious day this is for our world.

We are so honored that Jennifer Devore has chosen to bless us with the grace of her presence. I know some of you may be shocked to see me. Let me assure you that I'm just as surprised as you are. The attempt on my life in Rome, as it turns out, was a successful one. I was betrayed by my wife and my so-called friends. I did, in fact, die. I was given a tour of Kolasi, but I'm so fortunate that Jennifer, in her ultimate wisdom, determined that my work here was incomplete. I think all of you who have previously followed the teachings of Thysia will agree that the only thing better than healing . . . is resurrection."

Ukweli looked around the room and saw the uncertainty in the faces of his closest allies and the people he loved the most. He knew they needed his strength at this moment, but he had just as many questions as everyone else.

"Alexander, Kelley, do either of you have a clue as to what we're dealing with here?"

"If Jennifer Devore is here," Alexander said, "then they have instituted the Dragon Clause. I'm just not sure what could have prompted it or what their target might be."

Ukweli's expression twisted between confused and concern. "What is the Dragon Clause?"

Alexander took a deep breath. "I was taught about Jennifer Devore and the Dragon Clause in preparation for being camerlengo to Invictus. It was presented as some sort of urban legend, and I didn't take it seriously."

"What do you remember about it?"

"Jennifer Devore is an eternal. She served evil and was ejected from heaven. Since then, she and the one she serves has sought to grow their influence on the earth. They monitor the hearts and minds of humans to eliminate credible threats to their power. They institute the Dragon Clause when they identify a target."

"Dammit."

"What is it UK?"

"It's Pax. Pax is the target."

"How do you know?"

"I had a dream that a dragon was chasing Pax. It was the same red dragon that was on the flag before the broadcast started. I woke up just as the dragon was about to devour him."

Kiera's countenance changed from fear and shame to disgust and anger. "You knew that Pax was in danger and you didn't say anything?"

"Kiera, I'm still not sure what kind of danger Pax is in. I don't even know why Pax is their target. What would they have against a baby? I don't expect an actual dragon to come after him. You should all be careful though. The Company sent a hit squad after me last night. I wouldn't have made it out had Unity not been there."

Paul balked, "Who is Unity?"

Ukweli looked around the room for Hope to explain that Unity was her sister, but she was no longer in the room.

"Honestly, I'm not sure. I'm glad she's on our side though. I'll check in with my parents to see what they can tell me about Jennifer and the Dragon. We'll reconvene soon. Until then, stay safe. Let me know if you have plans to leave the country. No one travels alone."

(7)

IMPERIUM
INTERGALACTIC

J ackson Connaught sat in his father's office in Islington. He was having trouble understanding his new role in the Company or Imperium Intergalactic or whatever they were called now. He just wanted to know how quickly he could have Ukweli Aseyori's head on a platter. There was a time when he had a great deal of respect for Ukweli. He never considered him a friend, but he always saw him as a worthy opponent. Now, however, Ukweli was a great threat to the Company and Jackson demanded immediate action.

"I don't see why we can't just go to Atlanta and put a bullet in his head!" Jackson paced the floor with nervous energy and flailed his arms in frustration.

"It's not that simple Jackson." Jennifer's patience with Jackson's uninformed aggression was growing painfully thin.

"Sure it is. We send in a team, they kill him, dump his body in the ocean, problem solved."

"We sent a team last night. None of them survived."

"Then send another one! He doesn't deserve to live!"

"Jackson, you're taking this too personally."

"Of course I am! What did you expect? He defiled my wife and destroyed my family and my future!"

"Jackson, you are my DayStar for a reason. I need this to be personal enough that you maintain your resolve, but not so personal that your recklessness ruins my plans.'"

"Then maybe you should've chosen another . . . DayStar or whatever. I want them to pay for everything I've experienced!"

"Jackson, Ukweli's union with the girl was ordained. There was nothing you or either of them could've done to change that. We need to focus on winning this planet and building our army. Only then can the Dragon claim victory for us. I've anointed you to lead. So go lead."

Jackson Connaught toured the world, beginning in Europe, city by city, to do the work of building an army that the dragon could lead against the weapon. Endowed with the power of DayStar, he performed miracles and granted blessings that attracted the downtrodden and the very desperate, along with the greedy and opportunistic. There was always a crowd of interested onlookers who provided the word-of-mouth publicity essential to the success of Jackson's recruiting efforts. Every time he spoke in public, he paid tribute to Jennifer Devore as the authority of the galaxy, he decried the Church of the Seer, which he described as defunct, and he urged the citizens to join the Company in their efforts to defeat the coming threat.

NOVEMBER 5, 2044

Ukweli sat at the desk formerly occupied by Remington Cross in the executive offices of the Church of the Seer. Whether by miracle, coincidence, or providence, the substantial resources allotted to the Church of the Seer had been overseen by Kelley, who now sat at the conference table beside Alexander, and across from Ukweli, as the trio sought to understand their new mission. The Church of the Seer was a one-thousand-piece puzzle that had been unceremoniously dumped onto the living room carpet, awaiting assembly.

There were several events or occurrences that the rebranded organization would have to consider. First, each of the three had personal yet varying encounters with Thysia and none of them knew exactly what that meant. Next, it was obvious that Thysia's personal involvement in the events in Rome prompted Imperium to change methods, perhaps even enter into a new phase, which drew the attention of higher, and possibly more sinister, leadership. If efforts to reorganize the Church of the Seer were to be fruitful and appropriate, the missions would need to reflect the motivations and abilities of the new opposition more accurately. Last, and most important to Ukweli, they needed to figure out why Pax was the Dragon's target. Alexander wanted Pax to increase in influence to draw the masses to Thysia. Kelley wanted Pax to become the most efficient and effective form of whatever weapon he was destined to become. Ukweli didn't see a weapon when he saw Pax. He only saw his newborn son. Ukweli just wanted Pax to be safe.

Ukweli, of course, had the added concern of trying to maintain the juggling act of balancing being Ava's husband and the father to Kiera's son. He loved Ava and he loved Kiera. Ava loved him and Kiera loved him. He needed them and they needed him. He managed the relationships like navigating a minefield, realizing that every step could be that much closer to success or the end of it all. He had no idea how Ava and Kiera had gotten along so well since they got back to Atlanta, but thought it unwise, and perhaps irresponsible, to go rocking the boat.

Alexander spoke up first.

"UK, we really must consider the possibility that, because of Thysia's direct actions in Rome, Imperium enacted the Dragon Clause as a prequel to war. Jackson is practically on a worldwide recruiting tour as we speak. The people are responding to his new powers, and it won't be long before he arrives in the states."

"Do we know what this coming war has to do with Pax?"

Alexander paused before speaking. "If I remember my training correctly, the purpose of Imperium is to grow evil influence in the world. They want to defile and violate God's creation. If Pax is the key to defeating Imperium, that is why the Dragon will pursue him. I honestly don't know exactly what his role might be though, other than the fact that he is some kind of a weapon that poses a threat to them."

"Look, we don't know how much time we have," Kelley joined. "Jackson is crisscrossing the globe and his followers are growing every day. I don't know what your golden child can do, but whatever it is, we need to figure out how to use it."

"Kelley, Pax is not a soldier and he's not your damn science experiment. He's a baby."

"Enough you two. Let's not turn on each other on day one. Listen, Pax will be ready when the time comes, until then, we need to do some recruiting of our own. It is my life's work to spread the good news of the power of Thysia and that is the message that will ultimately open the eyes of those blinded by the counterfeit prosperity of Imperium."

"I agree that we have to recruit, but how can we spread a message when Imperium has active control of the outlets and the Internet?"

Kelley began to smile. "Hey, have either of you guys seen *Hamilton*, the old stage show?"

Alexander shook his head no. Ukweli tried to remember if he and Kiera watched it together in Islington.

"What if we wrote a series of letters and distributed the information on paper? It's old school, but it might be what is required now."

NOVEMBER 8, 2044

Jennifer Devore announced that, given the corruption and election tampering sponsored by the terrorists from the Church of the Seer and its sympathizers, there would be no federal elections and President James would be inaugurated for a third term in January.

NOVEMBER 20, 2044

The first few weeks after Jennifer announced the repeal of the holy book ban, church attendance showed no measurable increase. The thought was that it would take some time for the citizens to trust the validity of the law change. It had only been fifteen years since the Dark Reveal and the majority of the citizens lived through the changes. It would take a while to adjust to the return.

However, the overwhelming majority of citizens didn't skip church services because of fear or skepticism, but apathy. People simply got used to not going to church. Once the population grew accustomed to "Sunday Funday," it showed no desire to return to the days of suits, dresses, and services.

⑧

ISLINGTON

NOVEMBER 21, 2044

Ukweli, Ava, Alexander, and Kelley were on board the jet, in transit to London. The team decided the information they needed was greater than the potential risk of meeting with Kobe and Mara. Even in the days prior to the Vatican, Ukweli's relationship with his father was strained, and Mara had already used surrogates Hope and Unity to communicate with Ukweli and protect him. They hadn't had a meaningful conversation since before Uzuri was killed, though, and Ukweli doubted they ever would, but with Pax's life on the line, he decided it was time to mend broken fences. The group landed at the airport in London and made the short drive to the family home in Islington where Ukweli spent his teenage years. They never had a domestic staff when Ukweli lived in Islington, but the house was now run by a group of men and women, all dressed in red, who invited Ukweli and his team inside. His parents were still at the university but were notified of his presence and planned to leave work early to join him and his guests for dinner and tea. While they waited, Alexander and Kelley went through the study, the art gallery, and the library, and marveled at the collection the Nobel laureates had amassed. Ukweli and Ava went into his old bedroom. He hadn't lived there since he moved to the Green Wood area of London at nineteen and was surprised to find it completely empty. There was no furniture, no electronics, and even the floors and walls had been stripped and recently replaced. *Maybe they're gonna turn it into a gym*, he thought.

Ukweli stood in the middle of the floor and closed his eyes and allowed his mind to drift. Ava turned toward the door and left the room. Alone, Ukweli began to play back memories of the time he spent in the room, studying with Kiera, playing video games with Adam and Paul, watching videos on football training. The more he thought, the lighter he felt, to the point that he felt like he was floating in midair. He visualized himself practicing his jujitsu and his kendo and working with his squash paddle. He remembered writing a poem to his sister and finding a creative solution to a difficult physics problem. The more he thought, the better he felt. The better he felt, the further he imagined himself so free, he floated from the floor.

Kelley, having left the library, walked into Ukweli's old bedroom and was stunned to see him glowing and producing pulses of electrical currents from his body as he levitated eight inches off the floor.

"UK!"

Kelley's voice startled Ukweli as he opened his eyes in time to see the room from a raised perspective just before he crashed back down to the floor. The fall was only a short distance but was so awkward, he fell and rolled once he hit the floor.

"UK, what was that?"

"I don't know. I've never done it before."

"What were you doing?"

"I was just standing here, thinking about the good times I've had in this room. I started to feel free and powerful, and I felt like I was floating. I didn't know that I actually WAS floating."

"You were producing some kind of energy. It looked like electricity."

"I don't know. I didn't feel anything."

"And you've never done that before?"

"Not that I'm aware of, no."

"Do you feel any different now?"

"No."

Kelley looked Ukweli up and down. "Cross said you had special abilities. I'm sure he didn't mean this though."

"He always said self-awareness is rare. I guess I'm still learning."

"Maybe you're just a weirdo."

"Little doubt there." They smiled.

Just then, Kobe and Mara walked in the front door and Ukweli and Kelley walked into the front room to meet them. After a simple but cordial embrace, everyone walked into the dining room where Ava had already been seated. One of the men in red retrieved Alexander from the library and escorted him to join the others. The staff prepared a delicious meal of sea bass with risotto and sautéed seasonal vegetables. The meal was so delectable that everyone ate in silence with no objections. It was only when the staff served the tea that Kobe broke the silence. "So, to whom do we owe this . . . this, the grace of your majesty's presence?"

"Kobe, please don't start." Mara rolled her eyes.

"No, Mara. It's obviously time for a celebration. Our prodigal son has returned home! Let's kill the fatted calf! Someone, quickly, fetch the signet ring."

Ukweli put his fork down. "It's okay, Mara. I know Kobe doesn't trust me. I understand the risks involved in coming here. I just really need answers and I didn't know where else to get them."

"Well, you'll get nothing from us! It is your hubris and recklessness that has us all in danger!" Kobe stood as he shouted.

"Kobe, sit down! Ukweli, please forgive your father, dear. He's been incredibly stressed at work lately and it seems that he's brought some of it home with him."

Ukweli sighed. "Listen, I don't want to stir up trouble for you. I'm sure that Ann or Jennifer is listening to us now. I just need to know what you know about the Dragon Clause."

"Wait, how do you know of the Dragon Clause?" Kobe spoke with a confused look on his face.

"I had a dream about it. Thysia gave Kelley a vision about it at the Vatican. Honestly, I'm still not sure exactly how Alexander knows about it. He did some studies about signs and symbols in a monastery so maybe that's where his answers come from. But we all know that it has something to do with Pax."

Kobe slowly sat and began to speak. "So, it's true. Son, I'm sorry. There's nothing we can do. The Dragon has immeasurable power and Jennifer has marked Pax as a great threat. Aside from that, Jackson has it among his goals to make you pay for your trespasses. You, Kiera, Pax . . . all of your friends—you're all in danger and there's nothing you can do to stop it."

Mara spoke directly to her son. "Ukweli, now is the time you must take all you have learned and you must begin to apply it to your life. This is a time when you must not only lead, but you must be willing to be led. I know you value your solitude, but now, more than ever, you need your friends, those who love you most. This is simply not a challenge you can meet alone. Whatever you do, hold on to Hope and Unity."

Four large men in red suits came into the dining room. The smallest of the men placed his hand on Ukweli's shoulder. "Captain Aseyori, your car is waiting to take you and your associates to the airport. Thank you so much for stopping by. For future engagements, please try to call first."

Ukweli shook his father's hand and gave his mother a long hug. He knew, and they knew, that this would be his last visit to his parents' home in Islington. He wasn't sure he would ever see them again and it broke his heart. Ukweli was completely unwilling to allow one shred of emotion to break through to the surface. A broken heart provides clarity. Suppressed emotions fuel focus. His friends needed a leader. He would be it.

9

THE POINT OF NO RETURN

NOVEMBER 22, 2044

Kiera finally decided to leave the house to enjoy the fall colors of the big trees in the park and for fresh air. Ukweli had given her explicit instructions to always let him know if she was leaving the house with Pax, but she didn't feel the need to bother him for just a short morning visit outside. Plus, she was already growing annoyed with Ukweli telling her what to do. She had never been the type to take orders.

Kiera unzipped her jacket at the top so the sun could sneak a peek at her chest and neck. There was something oddly satisfying about the mixture of the warmth of the sun and the cool air on her skin. Kiera sat calmly on the park bench and watched her parents entertain Pax in his stroller.

Ukweli is so dramatic, she thought to herself. *The real sin would be staying cooped up inside on a beautiful day like this.* She took a peek at Pax, still in his stroller, before allowing her head to lean back to take the sun rays head on.

After a few minutes, the warmth of the sun disappeared, and she felt herself in a shadow. She opened her eyes to see a large man dressed in red standing in front of her, blocking the sun. She quickly sat up and pulled her zipper to her neck. "Can I help you, sir?"

"I need you to come with me."

Kiera saw out of the corner of her eye that more men dressed in red had her parents bound and had taken Pax out of his stroller.

"What do you want with me? What do you want with my son?!"

"What I want is for you to close your mouth and come with me!" The man grabbed Kiera by both arms and lifted her off the bench. Fear and pain caused her to let out a short scream.

"Unhand me, brute!" Kiera kicked and flailed but she couldn't free herself. The man threw her to the ground.

"Listen, we can do this the easy way or the hard way. It doesn't matter to me."

Suddenly, Kei, now standing behind the man, said, "Since it doesn't matter." She sliced through the muscle in the man's lower legs, followed by blows to his back and abdomen, causing him to bend over. With a swift and decisive blow, she separated his head from his neck and his limp body fell to the ground.

Paul emerged and attacked both men with his sword still sheathed. He punched one and the other with powerful blows to the face and chest. Kei made her way to the skirmish and plunged her blade into the chest of one of the men while Paul secured Pax, just before a small twitch of his foot on the throat of an assailant snapped the man's neck, causing his active body to lie motionless.

Kiera's father untied himself and began to untie his wife.

She shook with fear but was physically unharmed. Kiera arrived, crying with bruised arms outstretched, reaching for Pax.

Paul handed Pax to Kiera and said, "Come on, we'll escort you home."

"Where did you come from?" Kiera continued to cry.

Kei placed a hand on Kiera's shoulder. "I hope you can understand that these are very perilous times for you and your family."

"Did Ukweli send you?"

"We are always watching."

"Thank you, for saving us." Kiera regained her composure. Throughout the entire engagement, Pax did not cry. Kiera placed him in his stroller, and he fell asleep.

DECEMBER 4, 2044

Ann Jefferson sat at the small table in the Aseyori's dining room in Islington and listened as Jennifer Devore revealed the plans for the future of Imperium to Kobe and Mara. There were six large men, all dressed in red, standing behind them while they listened intently as Jennifer explained their lives away.

"I need you to understand—okay, *need* is a strong word—but I want you to understand that none of this is personal. Imperium has greatly benefitted from your research and though your hearts have been perfidious, your resolve has remained firm. I really enjoyed watching your progress. But, alas, every beginning has an end, and the time has come for your final and greatest contributions to the movement. I sincerely thank you for your service."

Jackson emerged from a back room as Kobe looked up.

"Jackson, you can stop this. We had no idea that Ukweli was coming to London. We have served the Company too well for it to end this way."

"Dr. Aseyori, please. Don't sit there and beg while your wife remains calm. It's a bad look."

"Tell me. What can we do?"

"I would suggest . . . that you go with a smile." Jackson raised his hands and began a series of sinister laughs as a smoky, cloud-like silhouette of a dragon appeared behind him and his eyes became like fire as he absorbed the life energy from Kobe and Mara. As the two scientists grabbed their throats, struggling to breathe, their eyes rolled into the backs of their heads as a red and silver mist left their bodies and surrounded Jackson. He inhaled the mist as Kobe and Mara gasped their last and fell to the floor.

DECEMBER 5, 2044

Islington Five News:

In a strange and tragic series of events, Drs. Kabeyesi (forty-nine) and Unimara Aseyori (forty-eight) were strangled to death during an invasion in their family home in Islington. The couple's nine-year-old daughter, Uzuri, was killed during a similar invasion at their family estate on Lagos Island in Nigeria twelve years ago. The couple is survived by their son, Tottenham-football-star-turned-religious-zealot Ukweli Aseyori of Atlanta.

Ukweli, reluctant to bury Kobe and Mara in Lagos because of the growing threat of grave robbers, instead received permission from the chancellor of Germany to inter his parents at the city cemetery in Gottingen. The couple once spent six months lecturing at the old university in the city and there were more than a few nobel laureates buried in the Stadtfriedhof there. Hope appeared graveside in Germany to console and encourage him.

Ukweli handled the business end of the loss like a man, he was a solid rock, but there were times when he couldn't help feeling alone, like an orphan. Despite the attempts on his life and the increasing possibility of danger, Ukweli traveled only with his wife. Ava didn't say much on the trip to Germany. She thought it was all that he needed that she be there, so that's what she did. She knew him to be vulnerable, but she was proud of his courage in the days following yet another family tragedy. She honored him with silence for his stoic and workmanlike demeanor in the face of inner turmoil. Ukweli was pleased that Ava was there, and he was more pleased that he didn't have to say it.

When Ukweli and Ava returned to the states, they unpacked but didn't tarry. Ava went to spend time with her parents while Ukweli went to the house in Decatur to see Pax. When he arrived, Kiera's father was sitting on the front porch and graciously invited Ukweli in. Kiera's mother was in the front family room swapping out a precarious diaper being strained at all contact points. *The ultimate weapon against evil*, he thought to himself. Just as Ukweli was about to address Kiera's mother, Kiera herself emerged from a back room.

"Mummy, I still don't see—oh, hello, Ukweli! When did you get back from Germany?" She walked over and gave him a friendly greeting.

"Just now."

"And where is lovely Ava?" There was just enough sarcasm to make it amusing.

"She is visiting her parents. Hey, can I talk to you?"

"Sure. Let's go in the office."

Ukweli followed Kiera around the corner and into a small room with a computer desk, two office chairs, and a small couch. The rest of the space was taken up by books and family pictures. Jackson was in a few of them. Ukweli sat on the couch and Kiera sat beside him.

"UK, I'm so sorry about your parents. I'm sure this trip has been hard for you. You know if there is anything that you need . . ." Kiera stopped talking. She looked into his eyes and the dam of his chiseled, rock-hard countenance had cracked and broken and was now flooding his face with tears. Kiera adjusted her position so she was on her knees beside him, facing the rear of the couch and he was on her left. She gently nudged his head and allowed it to rest on her left shoulder. She rubbed his back with her right hand and his head with her left hand as she rested his cheek against hers. She had never seen him cry before, she wasn't entirely sure he ever had, and she suddenly felt a pillowy cloud of delight begin to rise in her chest as it occurred to her he had chosen to be vulnerable *with her*. Ukweli sat on the couch in the office in the house in Decatur and cried on Kiera's shoulder for four minutes. He eventually held his head up and used his shirt to wipe his tears away.

"UK, that's nasty. That shirt is too expensive for you to get it all snotty." She smiled and grabbed a couple of tissues from the box on the desk and handed them to him.

"I'm so sorry for coming to you like this."

"Don't be silly. You know that I'm here when you need me. Thank you for trusting me."

Ukweli looked at Kiera. Her light-brown eyes were soft and warm. She wore no makeup, and he noticed a sunny glow on her clear skin. She had on black yoga pants and an oversized t-shirt with a picture of Elton John that read, "Saturday Night's Alright," and her hair was in what she called a "struggle bun." He leaned in toward her and kissed her softly on the lips. He hugged her tightly and said, "I love you, Kiera."

She looked at him, shrugged her shoulders, and said, "Of course you do. I'm cool. I'm pretty. And I gave you a cute baby . . . so."

"Kiera . . ."

"I'm just saying." They laughed. "I love you too, UK." They kissed again and shared another long hug. As Kiera released Ukweli, she noticed he wasn't letting go.

"Hey, Ukweli, what are you feeling right now?"

He didn't respond. Instead, he sat back and pulled her toward him until she straddled him. She rested her hands on his shoulders. "I thought you said you were tired of . . . what did you call it? Moving in the shadows?"

"I guess you have more of a hold on me than I thought." They kissed again. This one longer and more passionate than the others. Kiera abruptly pulled away.

"UK, wait. You're vulnerable and I don't want you to do something you'll regret."

"I could never regret being with you."

"We can't keep doing this. You know I love you, but—"

"Hey, look into my eyes. I know where I am, and I know what I'm doing. Most importantly, I know who I'm with. I see you. Don't you know what you mean to me?"

"No, I don't, UK. Not always." Kiera removed the clip from her bun so that her hair slowly cascaded down to her shoulders.

"Not always?"

"No. You've never chosen me."

"You chose Jackson."

"UK, babe, you left me. You knew I loved you and you abandoned me."

"Nah, love. I didn't leave. *You* left. You followed Jackson to Atlanta."

"Hey, it would've taken a single word from you. That's it. One word and I would've stayed in London."

"I'm sorry I haven't always told you how I feel. So here, let me show you."

The couple walked out of the room together, holding hands, before Ukweli went to Kiera's mom and picked up Pax. He walked outside and sat on the porch swing. Kiera's dad was already on the porch in a rocking chair scrolling through football highlights on his phone.

"I'm sorry about what happened to your parents, son."

"Thank you, sir. They were good people."

"I hope you know Pax is perfectly safe here with us. We would never let anything happen to him . . . or to my daughter."

Except for the time you literally let something happen to him and your daughter. "Yes, sir, I know. Thank you for that."

Ukweli turned his attention to Pax, who had been quietly smiling behind a river of drool. "What a handsome young man you are." He bounced him up and down a few times before Kiera's father warned he had recently taken a bottle and it wasn't wise to shake him up.

Inside, Kiera's mom, troubled by the events of the day, offered unwanted advice.

"Kiera, dear, I know it's none of my business, but you really must regain control of that relationship."

"You're right, Mummy, it's none of your business."

"I just want what is best for you, Beta, and I promise you, he will hurt you. Look, I know you love him, and I know he is a perfectly nice boy, but you can't allow him to use you as a vitamin to supplement the deficiencies in his marriage."

"I won't turn my back on him."

"No one is asking you to. I just don't want you to get it in your head that just because he decides to dump his emotional sewage on you, that it somehow translates to true affection."

"Well, Mummy, regardless of how you think things are, he loves me, and he needs me right now. And I'm going to be there for him."

"Oh, sweet Beta, that's my point. He needs you *right now*. Please, just be careful. The heart is deceitful above all things."

10

THE POWER OF DAYSTAR

DECEMBER 20, 2044

Three men in black clothes with red jackets approached a large group of people that comprised a central Atlanta homeless community. This group congregated most days on the corner of Forsythe and Trinity, and they shared whatever they had and cared for one another. But today, they walked the block to the bus station on Brotherton, chasing the promise of a hot meal. The men in red jackets gathered fifteen or so members of the group around a black SUV with red interior and told them to wait for directions. Once everyone assembled, a man got out of the back seat. He was dressed in an all-red, three-piece suit, shirt, tie, and socks, with red and black cross trainers. The man summoned the group, motioning with his hands that they should come closer as he began to address them.

"Good evening, citizens. I hope you have all enjoyed a prosperous December Holiday season. It is certainly my honor to spend these last moments of your lives with you and, while you may not realize it yet, it is your great honor to spend these moments with me as well. Listen, everyone falls on hard times. I understand. Life has hit me in ways that none of you could begin to fathom. But I can make you this promise. The sacrifice of your meager lives today will help to usher in a period of unprecedented prosperity for your city. Look around you! They are just busy as bees, living lives that your sacrifice has made possible. They won't remember you. Hell, they won't even know you did this for them. Quite honestly, even if they knew, they wouldn't care. But do you know who cares? I do. I care. I care about you and it's important to me that you leave this existence knowing that someone cared."

One of the men in the group responded. "Hey, pal, I don't know about all of that. But your men told us you were inviting us to dinner."

"Oh, I'm so sorry for the misunderstanding. Thank you for agreeing to join me for dinner."

"Hey, aren't you the mayor?"

"Why yes, yes, sir, I am. My close friends call me Jackson." At that moment, his eyes became like fire and his body began to glow. Suddenly, there was a great flash of light and a large black cloud with red and gold streaks appeared behind him and began to materialize into a large dragon. As Jackson's power grew, so did the strength of the dragon who now appeared with greater detail with jeweled green eyes that sparkled in the sun and large strong wings that seemed to surround Jackson like a smoky forcefield. "But you can call me . . . DayStar!"

The dragon moved quickly through the crowd, simultaneously consuming the spiritual energy of each victim and asphyxiating their physical bodies. The people all reached for their throats and gasped for air as they rolled around on the ground like they were on fire. DayStar stood with his arms by his side and his face tilted upward as he absorbed the essence of each member of the community. He opened his eyes and took a deep breath, inhaling it all.

"Where to boss?"

"Decatur. I'd like to go home now."

DECEMBER 21, 2044

Ukweli assembled the team from their various locations around the globe. Everyone was pleased and moderately surprised to know that Paul and Kei had married during their time away. Adam spent his time in California, surfing and diving. Charlotte came back with the grim report that Jackson Connaught had not only been performing miracles and wonders, but had been steadily growing in power because of some sort of supernatural ability she was unable to explain.

Ukweli addressed the group.

"I've called everyone in because we seem to have a new adversary. Well, not new, but certainly improved. We have satellite footage of an interaction between Jackson and a group of city dwellers."

The team watched the stream as Jackson absorbed the group's life energy. The dragon was not visible on the screen.

"What sorcery is this?" Adam asked as he watched the screen. "What is he doing to them?"

"He is absorbing their essence," Alexander explained.

"It's the same thing that happened to my parents," said Ukweli. "Law enforcement in Islington thought they were strangled, but there were no signs of physical trauma to their neck area. The only bruising was on their extremities, the same as this group of victims."

Kei said, "Please help me understand what we're watching."

Ukweli took a breath. "When Jennifer Devore instituted the Dragon Clause, it gave Jackson the power of the DayStar. The dragon that has appeared in our visions? It's Jackson. And he's more powerful than we ever could've known."

Kelley said, "We need to kill Jackson before he becomes too powerful."

Ukweli responded. "That time has already passed. Jackson has been traveling the world using the power of the dragon to consume life energy. I'm not even sure how to kill him now."

"I can't wait to try," said Kelley.

Just then, Ukweli's phone began to buzz. It was Kiera.

"Hello. Kiera? Are you okay?"

"Kiera is just fine, UK. Oh, I am too, thanks for asking."

"Jackson?"

"Wow! It's so nice that you recognize my voice after all that's happened."

"If you hurt one hair—"

"Really, UK? I'm still exchanging pleasantries and you're already playing the hero? Geez, you are wound tight, my guy. Hey, I'm gonna call you on video chat so you can put me on the big screen. I wouldn't mind seeing the team."

Ukweli handed his phone to Charlotte, and she switched the call over to video chat and patched it through to the big screen in the office.

"Hello, guys! Oh wow! Everyone is there. I'm so glad to see you all. Look, I have a proposal for the Church of the Seer, and I wanted the whole team to be able to think it over." Jackson was eating a bag of salt and vinegar chips as he spoke.

"Any proposal that ends with me putting a bullet in your forehead sounds good to me."

"Ahh, Kelley, you were always my favorite. The classic femme fatale, beautiful and ruthless. I really wish I met you before I fell for my wife. We could've been quite the team."

"Jackson," Ukweli broke in. "Your proposal?"

"My bad, UK. You guys come out to the house in Decatur. We'll talk here. Go ahead and gear up though. My guys are pretty upset with you, and I wouldn't want you to be caught off guard. I'm not saying that something bad is gonna happen, but, you know, I'm not saying that it's not either. Anyway, Kiera's dad is cooking on the grill. Let's break bread and talk this out. See you guys in a few." The feed ended.

After a long pause, Charlotte said, "What the hell was that?"

"If Jackson has Kiera, then Jackson has Pax." Ukweli's face changed as he spoke.

Kelly responded, "Well, you heard him. Gear up. Let's go talk to DayStar."

"We've seen what he's capable of. He's trying to get us to let our guards down. Do not treat him aggressively, but don't lose focus either. We have no idea what to expect from him. Let's take care of each other. Alexander, stay close to Kelley."

"I always do, UK."

(11)

THE BLOCK
PARTY

The team arrived in two black SUVs at the house in Decatur to an unexpectedly festive environment. Jackson organized a December Holiday season-themed block party and there were twenty or so people from the subdivision in the house and the backyard. There was holiday music playing and children were opening elaborately wrapped gifts as they sat beside a holiday tree or in front of the mantled fireplace. There were decorations all over the house and there were large inflatable figures of Santa and Frosty on the front lawn that were much too obnoxious for the very conservative neighborhood.

Everyone got out and took in the scene. "What is all this?" Kelley was suspicious.

Ukweli addressed the group. "Go to comms. Something isn't right."

Each member of the group touched a blue light near their shoulder to sync communications and drew a weapon.

"Alexander, Ava . . . get these people out of here. Now."

As Alexander and Ava began to usher the crowd away from the house, a large man dressed like an elf approached the team.

"So, the Seers hate the December Holiday season so much you came all the way out here to ruin our block party?" As he spoke, he was joined by another fourteen men, equally as large and all dressed like elves.

"Where is Jackson?"

"DayStar is busy at the moment. I'm sure we can help you with whatever you need."

"I need you to get out of my way." Kelley ran toward the first man and, before he could lift his assault rifle, made three swipes with her sword across his chest and back. The others began to fire at the team as they dispersed and engaged. The team all fired weapons except Ukweli and Kelley, who both made their way through the group of large elves with the precision and tenacity of expert swordplay. One by one, they slid and slashed, releasing torqs into the atmosphere with the screeching hiss of tortured souls until all of the elves lay silent on the front lawn.

The team slowly entered the front door behind Ukweli. Once inside, they moved quickly from room to room, looking for Pax, Kiera, or any sign of Jackson. Once each of the rooms were checked and cleared, they went out the back door onto the porch and into the backyard. Alexander and Ava cleared the last of the people there, which included Kiera's father, who had been cooking hot dogs on the grill, completely unaware of the battle in his front yard.

Ukweli approached Kiera's father who just stared straight ahead. Ukweli waved his hand in front of his face, but Kiera's father did not react to Ukweli being in front of him. He just stood there burning hot dogs.

Ukweli lightly touched him on the arm. "Carlos, where is Kiera?"

Kiera's dad continued to stare straight ahead. He finally responded with a monotone low-pitched question. "Ukweli, why are you sending everyone away?" he said very slowly.

Ukweli turned him away from the grill and held both of his arms. "Carlos, this is very important. Where is Kiera?"

"She and Pax went with Jackson to get ice cream. He said they would be back, but he left you a surprise on the small grill over there. It's a brisket that he's been smoking all day."

"A brisket?" Ukweli walked over to the small grill and slowly lifted the lid. There was a loud digital click and the timer on the small bomb sitting on the grates of the grill started a countdown from five. "Bomb! Get down!" Ukweli ran and grabbed Kiera's father and fell on top of him to cover him from the blast as the other team members ran away.

It was a small blast that only destroyed the grill. It was designed for a small radius, for a single target. Just then, Ukweli's phone rang.

"Jackson."

"Hey, did you enjoy the brisket? Did I make it too spicy?"

"Where are you?"

"I'm just spending some quality time with my wife. Honestly, I'm starting to take it personally that you insist on interfering with my marriage at every turn. Please respect our privacy during these trying times."

"Dammit, Jackson. Where is Pax?"

"Oh yeah, I almost forgot about the ultimate weapon. Hey, he's fine. I'll raise him as my own. I'm sure I'll be a better example for him than you, well, with all of the violence and your womanizing and such."

"Jackson, don't do this."

"You couldn't beat me at Highgate. You couldn't beat me in Rome . . . at least not without cheating. Just face it. I'm better than you. I'm ten steps ahead of you. I have everything you want and there's nothing you can do about it."

"I'm gonna kill you when I see you again."

"C'mon, UK. I could've killed you just now if I wanted you dead. Don't be like that."

"I will kill you when I find you."

"Goodbye, UK. I wish you luck in all your . . . impossibilities."

The Great Eternal Paradox – Issue 1, January 1, 2045

Making Good Better?

When God created the world and said that it was good, it wasn't on a scale that suggests that it was good vs bad, or good vs great, or good vs just okay. God created all of existence with words; there was no time, space, or any resource materials. It would then be illogical for God to suggest that what was created was in some way superior to what had yet to be created. So, when God said that the creation was good, who else needed to be convinced? When you are the creator of a thing and you make it the way you want it such that it serves the purpose for which it was created, who has the authority to tell you they can make it better? Who has the power to question what God has made? If God has made something good, there is no human intervention or terminology that can improve on that. We don't have the responsibility or the ability to make the world better than God made it. We must, however, work to undo the damage we've already done. It honors God for us to appropriately steward resources.

JANUARY 20, 2045

President James was inaugurated to a third term in a small ceremony inside the Oval Office. No media was allowed but staff photographs of the event were made available online.

> *"I and I alone have the foresight to lead this nation, and thus the world, into the next stages of our development. I'm so very happy for you, that you have such outstanding leadership."*
>
> —President James in his inaugural address

JANUARY 28, 2045

Ukweli, Alexander, and Kelley sat in the office at the Church of the Seer. It had been over a month since Jackson took Kiera and Pax and there had been no further movement. Jackson hadn't made any public appearances and, though the team used its substantial worldwide resources, they had no idea where Jackson had gone. He had taken Kiera and Pax and disappeared without a trace.

"You know, he could be anywhere in the world right now. How are we supposed to stop him? We can't even find him." Kelley was obviously frustrated.

Alexander added, "Well, with the powers of DayStar, he may not even be restricted to this world."

"What is that supposed to mean?" Ukweli looked puzzled.

"Theoretically, DayStar would have powers to travel between worlds, possibly even between dimensions."

Kelley sighed. "You're making my head hurt."

Ukweli spoke. "If he has the power to travel within dimensions, how can we find him? Dammit, I wish my mom were here now."

"This may be a peculiar suggestion, but since we're dealing with unknown dimensions, maybe it's time to consult someone who communicates on unknown planes."

"What are you talking about, Alexander?"

"I'm saying that there is a woman who lives in the Underground who might be able to help us."

"Are you saying that she can talk across planes?" Kelley had a look that reflected that she was annoyed but slightly entertained.

"I don't know, Kelley. Maybe she can. Look, we've tried everything else. What could it hurt?"

Ukweli thought for a moment. "I haven't been to the Underground since my last mission at the warehouse there. They may not welcome me with open arms."

12

THE NECROMANCER

Ukweli, Kelley, and Alexander walked through the Underground trying to draw as little attention as possible. They found it difficult, though, to seek aid in finding someone who doesn't want to be found, without arousing suspicion. Everyone in the Underground is looking for something specific, but most folks who would have to go to the Underground to get what they need already know where to go. If there are two things that the Underground dwellers don't take kindly to, it's outsiders and questions. Since Jackson's emergence as DayStar, all psychics, madams, prophets, and soothsayers had gone into deep hiding, and no one was exactly sure why. But locating the Necromancer was proving to be a difficult task. Finally, after some bartering and bribing, the group came upon a door that once represented the entrance to a hip Asian fusion restaurant and sushi bar.

Kelley knocked on the door. A very small, very old woman in a purple hooded gown covered in jewels opened the door.

"Yes, how may I help you?"

"Do you know why we're here?" Kelley asked.

"Child, whom do you seek?"

Ukweli answered, "We seek an audience with the Necromancer."

"There is no one here by that name. But please, come in and sample our exotic fusion tea. It will help to calm some of the aggression that you carry, dear. My apologies, but the two of you will need to wait outside."

Kelley and Alexander looked at each other as Ukweli cautiously followed the old woman inside. It was very dark as the only light was provided by decorative candles in the shapes of safari animals, zebras, giraffes, rhinos, and the like. The smell of incense flooded the room. There were no fewer than five of them lit, providing aroma and plenty of smoke that made an already curious scene seem creepy.

"Son of Nigeria, please have a seat. Your tea will be ready momentarily."

Ukweli kept his hood over his head. Though he was no longer concerned about trying to conceal his identity, he thought it wise not to expose more than he was asked. After a few moments, the old woman returned with a smoking glass of liquid and a small glass tray with some herbs.

"You may use as much or as little as you prefer. This being your first visit here, I would tread lightly should you require your faculties."

"This is fine. Thank you."

"Oh, good. That will be eight hundred dollars. Cash only please."

"Eight hundred dollars for a cup of tea? Perhaps I wouldn't mind the herbs after all." Ukweli paid the old woman, and she disappeared through hanging-strings of beads. After three minutes, she reappeared.

"DuaTre will see you now. Please be respectful. Follow me."

Ukweli followed the old woman through the strings of beads and down a hallway that seemed much too long for a dwelling this size. It was also very narrow and Ukweli couldn't help but think that the building plans couldn't have possibly been approved by the local fire marshal.

The old woman eventually led Ukweli into a dark room lit by just two candles. She instructed him to take a seat in the chair. It was made of wicker, and he was impressed when he sat that it was sturdier than it looked. Once Ukweli was seated, his guide turned around and left the room, closing the door behind her. Ukweli sat facing a bean bag chair and the only other furniture in the room was a small bed in the corner and the two small tables that held the two burning candles. The walls were blank and there were no windows. The door opened behind him.

"Hello, Ukweli. I apologize for the delay."

Ukweli was surprised that he was now being addressed by a small girl, perhaps age five or six. She walked briskly into the room and plopped onto the bean bag.

"Excuse me? How do you know my name? And aren't you—?"

"Would you really listen to my words if I had to ask your name?"

Ukweli removed his hood. "How is it that a girl of your age is in possession of cosmic knowledge?"

"You are only able to perceive me this way. It is how I can assure my safety. Things have become very dangerous for our community these days."

"Why are things more dangerous for you? What has changed?"

"The Dragon has been hunting and consuming the life energy of necromancers to absorb their abilities. I know you to be an enemy of DayStar so I will help you get what you need."

"And what is it that I need, girl?"

"You will first need to change your tone. Remember, I'm not the child you see. I'm here to help you on your way, but what lies ahead of you are very dark and difficult tasks. I am not, in any way whatsoever, obligated to help you. But you will need what I have to offer should you be successful in your quest to rescue your loved ones."

"My apologies. Please, advise."

"That's better. I can admit that you are very easy on the eyes. And you have an inner strength that you still must learn to properly express. You can't reserve your toughness for times you are angry. I can see why she is so committed to you though."

"You speak of Ava? My wife?"

"It is curious you thought of her first. I know you experience inner turmoil concerning your divided love interests. Most powerful men would just enjoy the bounty, yet you experience guilt."

"Ava loves me and gives me the support I need to get things done. She is like a foundation made of solid rock. But I have loved Kiera since I was a boy in London. She has been the object of my desire for many years. And now she is in trouble, along with my son, and it's my fault."

"Surely, you are correct, but now is not the time to assign blame. You can get to your light and your child, but you will need everything that your wife offers you. She is the key to your future and, I fear, our future as well."

"Please, tell me what I have to do."

"The information that you seek can only be accessed by communing with those inside the Astral Plane. For this, you will need to consult Bing Ren. He is a guru who lives in solitude at the summit of Gasherbrum on the border of China and Pakistan. The air is too thin and too cold for any other human to exist there for more than a few moments without aid. You cannot gain an audience with Bing Ren unless you approach him with two artifacts that are specific to your request."

"What artifacts?"

"You will first need to access the shipwreck on the shallow ledge in the Cayman Trough and retrieve the Captain's Goblet from the desk in the belly of the pirate ship *Genesis*. Take care, as he will not let it go willingly. There are large creatures who guard the ship and they feed on nonorganic materials. You will have to make the dive without aid. The pressure is great, and you will be surrounded by unknown entities, frigid water, and complete darkness. You must count on Thysia to guide you so this will be the greatest test of your faith."

"And the second item?"

"You must walk the burning sands of the Gobi Desert to the oasis where the Black Swan sings. There, you will find water that is able to cleanse the body and the soul. But beware, there are marauders all over the desert looking for great spoils. Therefore, you cannot use air or ground transport. The only way to avoid detection is to make the trip into and out of the desert on foot."

"Desert water. Got it."

"Once you make the climb to Bing Ren and present him the water in that artifact, he will grant you access to the information you'll need. Beware his beast who serves as both guide and protector. The beast will judge your heart and she devours those with lowly agendas."

"Sounds pretty straightforward."

"Ukweli, time is of the essence. Until you retrieve and activate the weapon, the world will continue to descend into the Great Madness and your friends will suffer in your absence. There is nothing more that your team can do for you. The path is for you and you alone. Every time you begin to question yourself, the world will suffer. Every stop. Every pause. Every hesitation leads to greater suffering. The key to your success is consistency. Go and never stop. You must work through the pain. The fear. The bitterness. The loneliness. The oppressive opposition. None of that will serve you now. Focus on the love. And whatever you do. Do not stop. The moment you think you are there, you are not. Keep going. Do not stop. Men throughout human history have had their ordained moments. This is yours. Everything you have experienced in your life until now has been for this moment. You are uniquely prepared for this. Do not stop."

The Great Eternal Paradox – Issue 2, April 2, 2045

Desperate Times?

What do you do when you've done all you can? This question is misleading. The real truth is that you've never done all you can. Don't ever give up the fight! As darkness closes in and madness like a tsunami breaks on the shore of your sanity, don't give up! Keep fighting! Take one more step. Throw one more punch. Fire one more shot. Who knows when the light will appear? It may be right around the corner. Regardless, now is not the time for neutrality. Those who sit on the sidelines in this fight may as well fight for the enemy. Your souls will be required just the same. Love. Encourage. Pray. Fight! Do not grow weary in well-doing!

13

THE GREAT MADNESS

APRIL 19, 2045

As spring approached in the city, most citizens looked forward to longer days, warmer weather, and the eventual return of bright colors to the landscape. Trees, no longer barren, once again produce green leaves that generate life-giving sustenance. Flowers bloom. Heavy winter coats give way to light jackets as the warm spring sun bathes the horizon, awakening the sleepy foliage.

This spring wasn't like that. Darkness gave way only to dense gray clouds that looked like they held water, yet it rarely rained. There was only gloom. More and more torqs were going rogue. Rogue torqs harmed themselves and others until their minds eventually gave way to the corruption and the result was always a violent rampage until the host collapsed into itself. The darkness accelerated the process and the planet seemed to descend into chaos.

It was the beginning of the Great Madness.

Kelley sat up in bed and stretched to welcome a new day. The room was still dark, and she thought it odd for the time of day. *Surely it is nine by now.* She checked her phone. 10:30 a.m. "Wow," she said. "I really slept in today. Alex!"

"In the bathroom, dear." Alexander's voice was muffled by his toothbrush.

"Why is it so dark? And it's cold in here." Kelley put her feet on the floor and reached for her robe. She walked to the sliding doors that open to the balcony and pulled back the drapes. "Uhh, Alex . . . why does it look like 10:30 p.m. at 10:30 a.m.?"

Alexander walked into the bedroom from the bathroom, carrying a towel, still drying his face. He held his head up from the towel and looked through the glass doors. "Oh no."

"What is it?"

"It's the Great Madness."

"What does that mean?"

"It's the last step in the Dragon Clause. It means DayStar is progressing. Come quickly. We need to find the others."

Ukweli and Ava stood on the deck of a large cargo ship in relatively calm waters in the Caribbean Sea. They both knew there would be no light at eight hundred feet below the sea surface, but they thought by going out in the middle of the day, they could maximize the available sunlight during the dive. They were surprised when there was no sunlight at noon.

"DuaTre said the team would suffer. I hope this isn't the beginning of whatever that means. It feels evil, but this is no time for distractions."

"UK, the wreckage is below us, but it sits on the edge of a

shelf and the drop-off from the shelf is two hundred feet. If you don't get the artifact and you feel the ship slipping from its position, just let it go. We'll have to figure out another way."

"Another way? If there's another way, we need to figure it out now!"

She deadpanned, "There isn't another way."

"It will take me nine minutes to dive to the wreckage, assuming that I'm actually diving toward the wreckage and that the creatures don't decide to have me for lunch."

"DuaTre said that the creatures only eat nonorganic materials, correct?"

"Ava . . ."

"UK, this is an impossible task. There's no way you can hold your breath for twenty minutes while performing this dive. We know that. We also know that DuaTre said that Thysia would help you. This is your destiny."

"Ava . . . listen, if I don't make it back . . ."

"Cut the crap, UK. The world is being covered in darkness. We don't have time for this."

"I don't know how long . . ."

"UK, it doesn't matter how long it takes. I'll be here when you get back. I promise you. I'm not going anywhere." She pulled his naked body close to her and kissed him deeply. "Now get your ass in that water."

Ukweli walked to the front of the ship and climbed over the edge. He turned and looked back at Ava in time to see her blow him a kiss. He grabbed it and smiled. Then he jumped.

The water was chilly but not cold. The sea seemed calm from the boat, but even small waves feel big when you're suspended in the middle of the ocean. *I'm coming for you, Pax.* Ukweli took a deep breath and disappeared beneath the surface.

Alexander and Kelley sat in their living room in front of their television, waiting for the others to join the video conference call. Paul and Kei joined the call together from Kei's family home in Sapporo. Adam joined the call from Carlsbad. Charlotte joined from Cairo.

"Yes, it's happening here too. Complete darkness." Kelley took a sip from a ceramic mug containing boiling water and a beef-flavored bouillon cube.

"Have we heard from the mission?" Paul asked with genuine concern in his voice.

Alexander responded. "No. We know they are in the Caribbean, but we have no idea if UK has even begun the first mission."

"It's impossible, you know. A free swim to eight hundred feet would be a world record and, somehow, we're expecting UK to swim to eight hundred feet, rummage around on a shipwreck, naked and in complete darkness, and then swim *BACK*?" Adam expressed his doubts.

"Not to mention the creatures that protect the wreckage. Just because they don't eat organic materials doesn't mean that everything under that water has the same diet." Kelley had questions too.

Alexander spoke up. "Is everyone okay? Adam, Charlotte, I really wish you guys weren't alone during the Madness."

Adam responded. "Well, I haven't been alone much, but I understand your concerns. It's only been dark here for a few hours and it's already getting bad in the streets. If it makes everyone feel better, I'll head to Cairo and camp out with Charlotte there. Maybe we'll have heard from Ava by the time I get over there."

"You might want to bring a couple of your bimbos with you because you aren't touching me with those wrinkled saltwater hands." Charlotte had a matter-of-fact look on her face.

"See? That's not even what I meant when I said *camp out*."

"Yeah, we all know what you meant. I'll see you when you get here."

"Although, a couple of travel partners might not be a bad idea . . ."

"Hey," Alexander changed directions. "Take care of each other. We have no idea how long this process with UK will take and rogue torqs are already running wild. The longer this goes, the more dangerous it will be for all of us. Please mind your mental health and the well-being of your loved ones and pray for our friends."

Ukweli worked his way down, down into the depths of what seemed to be endless nothing. He concluded it was akin to what astronauts experienced in outer space. Of course, astronauts don't spacewalk naked, so the metaphor had limits. He was pleased, yet surprised, that the water below the surface was so calm. Calm, but dark. It wasn't very long before the lights from the ship completely faded and Ukweli could see nothing at all. He could feel ocean-dwelling creatures around him, some small, some not so small, but none of them bothered him and he certainly didn't feel the need to pause for a formal introduction. In times like this, to avoid distractions, it's best to keep things simple. Even a small, blue fish with a bad memory could remember simple instructions . . . just keep swimming. Don't stop swimming.

Two minutes into the swim, Ukweli began to feel the strain in his muscles. *It's far too early for this*, he thought. He decided he would take his mind off the act of swimming and try to notice his surroundings. He read that when humans lose a sense, the other senses become heightened. Now that he was basically blind, he decided to focus on what he could hear. Three minutes into the swim, the pressure was so great on his ears, he couldn't hear anything. He kept swimming.

Four minutes into the swim, doubt began to creep into his mind. *I'm going to die here in this ocean.* His arms began to fatigue, and he wondered how he still managed to hold his breath. If he were on the surface, he would've relieved his lungs long ago.

Five minutes in. Something very large swam by. It purposely grazed against Ukweli's body, as if to let him know he wasn't alone—but not in a comforting way. It felt like a warning shot. Of course, there were things that could swallow him whole swimming all around him. Suddenly, the darkness felt like a blessing. He just kept swimming. Farther and farther down.

Ukweli wasn't sure if he was fully conscience at this point. Seven minutes into the swim, he wondered if he were already dead. The burning in his lungs assured him he was alive. He had no idea how deep he was. It had been completely dark almost the entire swim. The water was extremely cold now. Ukweli was grateful for it though. He remembered sinking his body into a cold tub after a sweaty football practice in London, and the invigorating feeling that came from the contrast of his burning hot muscles and the icy water. He convinced himself that the cold temperature of the water was giving him aid as he swam. He didn't know the science and he didn't have any proof. It was a comforting thought though. He kept swimming.

Something very large with tentacles came over to say

hello. It wasn't an octopus, and Ukweli didn't feel any suction cups on the tentacles. The creature never put any pressure on Ukweli, it didn't try to drag him away and it never squeezed his limbs. It wrapped its tentacles around his right arm and his left leg and then unwrapped him and let him go. The tentacles themselves felt larger than human limbs so Ukweli knew the beast had to be massive. He was surprised at his own lack of fear at that moment. Somehow, he knew that creature was not there to harm him. It was as if he had just passed a checkpoint and had been approved for entry . . . like he just went through a deep-sea metal detector.

Ukweli knew he had been swimming, and holding his breath, for at least nine minutes. He could be two hundred feet away from the wreckage or it could be right in front of him. He was beginning to experience disorientation, and he wasn't exactly sure which way was down. That's the thing about being in complete darkness, there is no frame of reference. He decided he would just keep swimming.

Ukweli swam for another minute or two minutes or thirty seconds—he wasn't sure—before he felt his lungs giving up. The burning had now subsided, and his body had gone into survival mode. He honestly couldn't tell if he was breathing or not. Maybe he had already drowned. Maybe what he was experiencing now was some form of the afterlife, maybe he was in limbo waiting on the ancient spirits to judge his soul. DuaTre warned him not to stop. He hadn't stopped. He hadn't . . . stopped. He . . . kept . . .

Ukweli wasn't sure exactly when he lost consciousness or how long he had been suspended in the depths of the open ocean. He regained consciousness just in time to see the light. *So this is what death feels like,* he thought. He knew the light was coming toward him because he did not have the ability to move.

His limbs were just dangling, and it was all he could do to focus one eye on the approaching light. Who would greet him in the light? Maybe St. Peter. Maybe it would be his mom. Would Uzuri be with her? *Are they together now, waiting on me?* The more Ukweli thought of a joyous reunion with his mother and his sister, the more he felt a warm comfort in his soul. The light grew closer and closer and Ukweli welcomed it as he floated along. He certainly didn't have the strength to reach for it.

"Adam . . . Adam . . . check in . . . where are you?!" There was static in the comms.

"I'm still five miles out! These damn things are everywhere!"

"I'm coming to you!"

"No! Don't leave the camp. I'll let you know when I get closer. I'll need your help getting in."

"How are you on ammo?"

"Almost out. They're aggressive but not skilled. My blade will win the day. Hold tight."

Charlotte scanned the area from the tower cam, and it was plain to see that the torqs were moving toward her location. Either they were anticipating Adam's arrival, or they learned that she was there. Either way, she would have to fight. She was ready.

She opened the front door and lifted the main gate. A group of torqs noticed the noise and started moving toward the camp. She revved the engine on her bike and flipped her helmet shield down. She squeezed and rotated the gas handle and released the brake, catapulting her bike into the night. She drove with her right hand and shot with her left. The accuracy and tenacity created a symphony as she screamed while the demons hissed, leaving their host machines to collapse as they disintegrated into the dark sky. She drove and shot until she could make out the faint glow of the headlight on Adam's motorcycle.

"Let's go, slowpoke! Hit the gas!"

"Shut up and shoot! Get these things off me!"

Adam was coming in hot and bringing a tsunami of torqs with him.

"That is the worst parade I've ever seen."

"Yeah? Look at the gate!"

A large group of rogue torqs, twenty or thirty, congregated at the gate of the camp.

"I got this. Move your ass!"

"I'm squeezing liquid out of this handle!"

Adam zig-zagged around landmarks and caught up to Charlotte's position.

"Hey, when we get to the camp gate, just don't stop. Drive straight through."

Charlotte reached into her inner jacket pocket and pulled out two grenades. "Drive straight through!"

She put the grenades up to her mouth, pulled the clips, and threw them into the middle of the group of torqs. There was a flash of light followed by a crack. Adam and Charlotte drove straight through as demons hissed and host machines flew in every direction. The gate lifted quickly as the pair drove under and slammed shut behind them.

"So, this is Egypt?"

"Glad you could make it."

Ava stood on the deck of the ship and gazed out over the dark horizon. The sea was relatively calm, so the boat didn't sway much. The shipmaster came out onto the deck from the pit and handed Ava a hot cup of tea and placed a warm blanket around her shoulders.

"Mrs. Aseyori, has there been no movement from the water? No word from the captain?"

"No, not yet."

"It has been over an hour now. Surely . . ."

"Surely what?" Ava pulled out a pistol and placed the end of the barrel against his temple. "Surely what?!" She held the gun in one hand and the tea in the other.

"My apologies, ma'am. I'll wait inside. Let me know if you need—"

"Thank you, sir." Ava sipped the hot tea and returned her attention to the dark water. The shipmaster decided he should be prepared for her to jump into the water at any moment. He now believed she was prepared to go in to get Ukweli herself, should she determine it best. He didn't doubt she could do it.

Alexander sat on the edge of the couch with a deep, contemplative countenance. Kelley sat on the coffee table facing him with her hands on his knees.

"We don't have a choice, Alex. We're almost out of food as it is." She gently touched the side of his face.

"Yes, Kelley, I know. But it's chaos on the streets. I can't ask you to go."

"Look, we have two choices. Either we both go and camp at headquarters, or I go, alone, and get resources from headquarters and bring them back here."

"Kelley, it's very dangerous out there. I won't ask you to go alone."

"So, you're coming with me?"

"No."

"Alex, I'll put you on the back of the bike. If you see something scary, just shoot it. We'll be there before you know it."

"You know I've never shot a gun. I've never taken a life."

"Desperate times, Alex. I'm gonna go gear up. Put on a coat."

(14)

THE EXCHANGE

Jennifer Devore sat behind the desk in the plush office at the Connaught Hotel in Manhattan. Behind her was a large portrait of Wellington Connaught, Charles's great-grandfather and founder of the original Connaught Hotel in London. He was dressed in a red military coat, though he never actually served in the British military.

"Charles, give us a bit of privacy please, dear, won't you?"

"Jennifer, please tell me where my son is."

"Charles, all I can tell you is that he is doing fine. Jackson has the weapon with him, and he is completely inaccessible to any earthly threats. At least for now. Please try to relax."

"Jennifer . . ."

"Charles?"

"Fine. I'll be right outside." Charles left the room with the disposition of a jilted toddler.

"Maybe we should go a little easier on him. He did lose his son once already."

"Goodness, Ann, are you losing your nerve?"

"No, I'm not losing my nerve. I just don't see how it benefits us to keep him in the dark."

"You're okay with literally every other human on the planet living in darkness, but you draw the line at Charles Connaught?"

"Good point. So, what is our next move?"

"All we can do now is continue to apply pressure and hope that the man fails."

"Is there no way we can intervene?"

"Not directly. Thysia has made it clear he will not remove the hedge from the man, the light, or the weapon."

"So, who exactly are we applying pressure to?"

"There is no such hedge around his friends. Darkness breeds fear and fear breeds doubt. With the entire world in darkness, as it descends into madness, we will certainly break the faith of many who currently believe."

"Have we considered the possibility that the darkness may drive some to a stronger faith in Thysia? Might it strengthen the resolve of some who believe? Or worse yet, might it drive some non-believers to a consideration of faith?"

"For those who are strong, it is not our goal to break their faith. We only want to crack the facade so that a sliver of doubt might creep in through the imperfections. If we can keep the lines blurred until the mission ultimately fails, the weapon will no longer be a threat. This world, and all its inhabitants, will be yours."

"What if the mission succeeds?"

"Then your fate rests with DayStar."

"And if he fails?"

"If DayStar fails, then we have failed. There will be consequences. The Beautiful One will be indignant."

"The Beautiful One knows Thysia has altered the rules to

favor the man. You would think the Beautiful One would understand, given that he, himself, has been unable to defeat Thysia?"

Jennifer stood up, walked around the office desk, and slapped Ann on the face, knocking her glasses to the floor. "You will not speak with such a free tongue concerning things you don't understand. Watch your mouth and stick to the plan. Get out."

15

FISK RENAULT

Ukweli opened his eyes. They burned, probably from the saltwater, but maybe from the stress of interpreting a new light source after so much darkness. Here, in the depths of the sea, eight hundred feet below the surface of the Caribbean, Ukweli sat in a chair across from a man, in the dry, candlelit, bowels of what was obviously a pirate ship. There was quite a bit of traditional pirate paraphernalia, feathered caps, pipes, treasure maps, and such. As Ukweli's eyes adjusted to the light, he noticed that the entire ship was surrounded by water, but he seemed to be in some sort of protective bubble. He couldn't see the bubble, but there was a visible line created by the pressure as the bubble held back the furious ocean. Ukweli sat up in his seat and took a deep breath. *You really don't think about breathing until you can't breathe.* His arms and legs were exhausted but recovering. He was just getting his bearings when the man in the room spoke.

"Hello, sir. And who do I have the pleasure of addressing?"

"My name is Ukweli Aseyori."

"East African?"

"I was born and raised in Nigeria, but my mother was from Tanzania."

"Swell. Welcome to the Caribbean. I'm Fisk Renault and I'm the captain of this ship. Her name's *Genesis*. Jenny for short. Four hundred years ago, me and my crew ruled these seas. We were the most feared sailors that ever left land. We talked the biggest talk and we had the biggest guns to back it up and everybody feared us because we had the fastest ship. We've been in battles all over this sea and no man-made vessel could ever dream of sinkin' us. We raided rivals, took their riches and their lasses, and sent 'em home broke, till one day I reckon ol' Poseidon just had enough. Biggest storm rolled in out of nowhere and made waves mast high. I made a deal with the devil to spare my crew, but a good captain goes down with his ship. And this is where I've been since. But I swear, in all my comin' an' goin', and in all my doin' an' seein', I ain't seen nothing like the sight of a naked you floatin' toward my Jenny. So, there're a few things you oughtta know. You're dead—well, mostly anyway. You swam by 'em once. You won't get to swim by 'em again. Even if you made it by 'em, you can't do what you did again. Whoever helped you get here better help you get back."

"Your deal with the devil . . . was it worth it?"

"I'd always do anything to save my crew. But they all died anyway so maybe the devil ain't much for promise-keeping."

"Do you know why I'm here?"

"I'd say you're here for my chests of doubloons, but that's hardly what a man gambles his life for. I sense a greater purpose."

"Are you here to help me?"

"No, I'm here to judge you. You prove worthy, you get what you came for and go home."

"And if not?"

"You stay here with me for a couple hundred years."

"What's the medium?"

"Ain't no better way to test a man's mettle than to put a sword in his hand and ask him to save the world."

"And how many fights have you had in the last . . . four hundred years?"

"Don't you worry 'bout me, son. Fighting is what pirates do."

Fisk Renault reached under the desk and retrieved two dueling swords. He tossed one to Ukweli. "Plus . . ." Renault smiled as he spoke. "I don't 'spect you've done much fightin' under the sea."

At that moment, the bubble collapsed, extinguishing the candlelight and enclosing the area in salt water and darkness. Ukweli desperately inhaled and clumsily adjusted the sword in his hand. Before he could react to the water pressure, he felt a sharp pain in his left thigh, immediately followed by sword slashes to his right arm, his right hamstring, and his left shoulder. He spun around in the water and flailed his sword around, but he could tell he wasn't hitting anything. Visibility was zero. The cold water was a shock to his system, but the water temperature and the pressure slowed his bleeding. Ukweli once again heard the voice of Fisk Renault.

"There're pretty big sharks at this depth, son. I guess they'll know you're here pretty soon, what with the way you're leaking fluid."

Ukweli continued to swing his sword through the water wildly, hoping he would connect with something other than the chair or the wall. There was another sharp pain in his right calf and again just above his right knee.

"Hospitality ain't never been my strong suit, but I got a lot of stories to tell, so at least I'll keep you entertained down here."

Ukweli stopped swinging his sword and was still in the water. He could hear Fisk Renault clearly, but it was only when he was still that he began to realize . . . he could *feel* him. *Of course*, Ukweli thought to himself. *Fisk made a deal with the devil. I can sense him.* Ukweli closed his eyes and focused on Renault's movement through the water. He could tell he was approaching in a curved pattern, similar to the aggressive attack pattern of a large shark. Ukweli felt his skin tighten on his right side and put up his sword to block the charge.

"Whoa, lucky defense, maggot. It's my fault for playing with my food. Now it's time to say good night, son."

Fisk Renault turned quickly to charge right into Ukweli's chest. Ukweli reached out with his left hand, just under the attack blade, and carefully guided it past his throat. With his right hand, he made an uppercut, thrusting the sword through the upper chest and under the clavicle of Fisk Renault. Immediately, the bubble and the candle reappeared and both men crashed to the floor. Ukweli took a deep breath, refusing his urge to gasp. He quickly stood. Fisk Renault grabbed the handle of the sword and carefully slid it away from and out of his body. He let out a heavy sigh and allowed his head to rest against one of the legs of a nearby chair.

"Never has a land dweller got the best of ol' Fisk Renault. Good luck in your questin' boy."

From Ava's chair on the deck of the boat, she couldn't tell if the sky was dark because of some sinister cloud covering or if the Company's sorcery supernaturally blocked any attempts by sunrays to sneak through. The extended darkness was obviously deliberate, but the longer it lasted, and the longer her husband was under the water. It began to take its toll, and Ava's diamond-hard belief began to slowly dissolve. She had been listening to the online radio station's mix of songs by Johann Sebastian Bach and similar composers when Moonlight Sonata began to play. Ava's eyes began to swell with tears as her memories were flooded with thoughts of her and her husband soaking in tandem bathtubs overlooking the banks of Lake Constance in southern Germany while being soothed by Beethoven's Piano Sonata #14 in C-Sharp Minor. She never associated classical music with romance before then, and now that she was furiously sparring with the doubt in her mind, the song sounded less like a love ballad and more like a funeral march.

She stood and walked to the railing and tried to imagine she could see a star so she could make a wish. As she strained her eyes to try to see any movement, something caught her eye. She reached for her binoculars and scanned the surface in time to see a man clinging to a large wooden board.

"Light! Light! Shine the light there!" She pointed as she barked. Two of the large spotlights just above the steering room shifted up and to the left and illuminated an exhausted Ukweli barely able to squeeze the plank. Ava threw the binoculars down, removed her boots, climbed the railing, dove into the water, and began furiously swimming toward her husband. When she got to him, she wrapped her left arm around his body and began paddling toward the lowering litter. The crew raised the basket to the side of the boat and escorted Ava and Ukweli to the safety of the deck. The medical staff lifted Ukweli onto a gurney and whisked him to the sick bay. Ava followed closely. They got to the room, locked the gurney in place, and fitted Ukweli with an oxygen mask. Ava, still wet from her rescue swim, walked over to Ukweli and kissed him over and over before lying her head on his chest. By now, she was crying uncontrollably and mumbling, "Thysia brought you back to me. It's a miracle. He brought you back to me."

Ukweli lay on the gurney and took deep breaths of oxygen from the mask. He was sure he had never been this tired. It was a weird feeling to be full of adrenaline and completely void of energy at the same time. He was barely aware enough to notice that Ava was crying on his chest. He was surprised and deeply touched. He managed to move his left arm just enough to rest it on her back. In all the excitement, everyone, even Ava, failed to notice the small, metal cup in Ukweli's right hand.

(16)

THE BEAUTIFUL ONE

Jennifer Devore and Ann Jefferson paced nervously in the office at the Connaught Hotel in Manhattan. Charles Connaught sat in the chair behind the desk. He watched the ladies pace back and forth, and his anxiety grew with each step. Charles had been fully committed to the Company and Ann Jefferson since the beginning. He was even supportive when Ann suggested that Jackson be inhabited, believing it to be the best way to ensure his son would manifest his full potential and, therefore, take the Connaught family name to greater heights. His arrangement with Ann would solidify his legacy for generations. Recently, though, there had been a chasm between he and Ann, and Jennifer's arrival only seemed to make things worse. When it came to planning or key decisions, Charles was often on the outside looking in, and now his patience and humility had become incredulity and cynicism.

"Exactly when will you two tell me what is going on?"

"When you need to know," Jennifer snapped with a sting-ing tongue and Charles sat back, sulking.

"Are you sure he's coming?" Ann wished she hadn't asked.

"When the man retrieved the first artifact, the Beautiful One decided we might achieve greater motivation with him here, with us, face to face."

"Greater motivation? Ugh."

"He said that he is coming to help us . . . to advise us."

"That's exactly why I'm here." Charles Connaught stood up, adjusted his tie, fixed the top two buttons on his sport coat, and continued to address the shocked occupants of the room. "I'm only here to help you succeed . . . and perhaps to . . . light a fire under the shapely rear ends of our leader-ship." When he uttered the phrase, "light a fire," he snapped his fingers and a small blue flame appeared above his now opened palm and disappeared when he closed his hand.

The two ladies immediately fell to their knees with their noses touching the antique Persian rug. Jennifer spoke first. "Beautiful One! Thank you for the honor of your presence! We worship the one true and living ruler of all!"

"Blah, blah, blah. Get up." The women stood. "Have I taught you nothing?"

"Sir? All that we know, we learned from you. For you are the ultimate source of truth and wisdom in the universe."

"Well, I can't tell. If I've said it once, I've said it a thou-sand times. Make a plan, then execute the plan. Period. You guys are all over the place. It's hard to tell if you're trying to conquer the citizens or unite them."

Ann was offended by the suggestion of incompetence. "We had them locked down before Thysia intervened. He keeps helping them. What do we do about him?"

"Thysia?! Please . . . he's just a two-bit magician with parlor tricks and whatnot. Besides, it's your fault that the Magician involved himself at all! It's your fault! If I've said it once, I've said it a thousand times. You must win with subtlety. When this species feels attacked, they don't walk, they run to the Magician. Your overly ambitious idea to unite the world under one religion planted the seed for resistance."

"But we controlled the resistance!"

"I would challenge you to mind your tone."

Ann Jefferson grabbed her chest and began to scream in pain. "Mercy, sir! Please! I beg for mercy!" The Beautiful One released Ann and she sat, trying to catch her breath.

"Please tell me why you have darkened this world."

Jennifer explained. "The darkness is in the playbook. We followed the plan. Plus, the citizens were beginning to lose respect for us. We needed to remind them that they have reason to fear us."

"And where is the subtlety in that? You wonder why the Magician is present? That's why! First, you allowed the churches to reconvene, then you challenged them with darkness and practically drove them to call on the Magician."

"Please tell us how to proceed, Beautiful One."

"The Magician has a hedge around the man, his light, and the weapon. The mysticism was ordained so we can't change that, at least not yet. The man will head into the desert soon, so our time is limited. Continue to challenge his friends with everything you have. See to it that they can't provide any support, should he need it. As for the rest of the population of this planet? Return them to a sense of normalcy and begin a more subtle plan of attack. Lull, divide, conquer."

"Of course, your grace. Thank you for your wisdom and your mercy."

The Beautiful One walked around the desk and grabbed Ann Jefferson by the shoulders and kissed her deeply. He then pulled Jennifer Devore to him and kissed her. "The mercy I have shown today will not be repeated. Bow down and worship your lord!"

Ann Jefferson and Jennifer Devore quickly dropped to their knees and began to sing a hymn of praise. The Beautiful One lifted his arms to receive the delectable, sweet energy. Suddenly, Charles Connaught collapsed to the floor, wide-eyed, exhausted, and confused.

The Great Eternal Paradox – Issue 3, June 4, 2045

You're capable of so much more than you know!

Moses, Jeremiah, and Gideon are just a few examples of heroes of the faith who didn't think they were capable of completing their assignment. We can look at their example and know that we're much more capable than we think! The enemy wants you to create a cloud of doubt, hoping to discourage you from pursuing your calling. God won't give you an assignment without equipping you for complete and total success! You can swim farther, jump higher, run faster, and endure more pain than you ever thought possible. The sun will shine again, and when it does, hit the ground running! It doesn't matter how dark the night gets, know that you have what it takes to conquer the day!

17

THE SUN RISES

Whoa."

"What is it, Alex?"

"The sun is up."

Kelley rushed out of the bathroom and entered the bedroom still brushing her teeth. "Does this mean they're giving up?"

"You know better than that, Kelley. It is good to see the sun again though."

Kelley stood in her bathrobe in the window and watched the sun peek over the tree line. *Simple pleasures*, she thought to herself. Her serenity was abruptly interrupted by the beating on the bedroom window by a wailing rogue torq approaching insanity.

"Ahhh!" Alexander screamed in fear and immediately regretted allowing that sound to come out of him in front of Kelley. "What is that?!"

"It's a rogue torq. That's how they look just before they break." Kelley was speaking from the closet as she was grabbing her weapons. She emerged, still in her bathrobe, with a gun in each hand, and fired into the window at the grotesque figure trying desperately to break the glass. Both shots hit directly, and the figure fell from sight. "There's no way that was the only one. Get up and grab a gun. They're here."

Suddenly, the front door was knocked off its hinges and five disfigured, rogue torqs rushed in. Kelley heard the commotion and moved toward the front of the house. "Get a gun, now!" She leaped into action in the front room, opening fire on the unwanted guests. She moved swiftly and precisely, up and down, around furniture. The torqs moved quickly but sloppily, and they were no match for Kelley's agility or tenacity. She made quick work of the visitors and checked outside for others. As she went back into the house, Alexander emerged from the bedroom, gun drawn, hands shaking.

"Where are they? Just point me to them!"

"We're all clear, Alex."

"Are you sure?"

"Alex, put that gun down."

"You told me to get it, so I got it."

"Now I'm asking you to put it down."

"Kelley, maybe I would be more of a help to you in these hostile situations if you taught me how to properly brandish a firearm."

"Stop talking like that. Don't say stuff like *brandish*. Just say, 'show me how to shoot a gun.'"

"Kelley, dear, will you teach me how to shoot, please?"

"I will. They'll be back. We need to call the others in. It looks like we're at war again."

Ukweli sat, fully reclined, in the large chair onboard the private jet. The plane was one of the many assets owned by the Church that added a great deal of convenience and comfort to the hyper-stressful environment created by the trials. Ava initially sat in Ukweli's lap, but now stretched her legs out and lay on his chest as he reclined. The two had been inseparable since leaving the Caribbean, mainly because Ava refused to let Ukweli out of her sight.

Ava loved Ukweli a great deal, but knowing how close she was to losing him to the ocean made her confront her true feelings and revealed how vulnerable she was. She was embarrassed she felt that way, but she couldn't help it. Knowing he had another mission, this one even more daunting and equally impossible, one that could take him from her, made her put aside her insecurities and embrace love without boundaries for the first time. She was no less committed to the mission. She would do everything in her power to see to it that Ukweli was successful. She did, however, accept the dose of reality that came with knowing that failure was possible and what that meant. She decided she would spend whatever time the two of them had remaining admiring his heartbeat.

The couple decided that it would be too risky to fly into Khanbumbat, so they headed for the Mongolian capital of Ulaanbaatar instead. The welcoming committee met Ukweli and Ava on the tarmac and invited them into the middle vehicle of the motorcade where they conversed with the Prime Minister.

"Good morning, Captain Aseyori. We're very excited for your visit to Mongolia. We have arranged for you and your beautiful wife to have a very authentic and enjoyable time here."

"Thank you, Mr. Prime Minister. We're very honored you would take the time to personally greet us here."

"We are well aware of the efforts you and your colleagues at the Church have made to ensure our safety on this planet. We are grateful. Also, Remington Cross was instrumental in our efforts to retain power here after an uprising in 2020 so we honor his legacy by honoring you."

"Thank you. Cross was an exceptional leader. I am curious though; what do you know of why I am here in Mongolia?"

"In my most recent meeting with my guru, I was given a vision of a battle for the souls of this world with a dragon on one side and a man standing opposite. My guru explained that I would have to help the man all I could, with certain obvious restrictions."

"Restrictions, sir?"

"The Gobi Desert isn't like most deserts on Earth. The majority of the vast landscape is rocky and easily accessible by motor vehicle. There are many animal and plant species that thrive in our lands and the Gobi is no different. Your biggest challenge in reaching the Black Swan would likely be the desert dwellers. They are known to be ruthless and extremely dangerous. That is where I can help you."

"You know of the Black Swan?"

"The Black Swan controls the commerce of the desert region and has grown in power in recent years because of their influence on world governments."

"How are they able to influence governments? What gives them this authority?"

"They control the oil wells in the desert and they have elite fighters all over the world to protect their interests. They are not unlike your Church, they just lack discipline and clarity. That is what Remington Cross provided for your organization—clarity. It's easy to stay focused when you know why you do what you do."

"How do I get to the Black Swan?"

"That's the easy part. He knows you're coming. You'll spend the next couple of weeks here with us in the capital and then we'll take you to him. He's looking forward to meeting you."

Ukweli and Ava spent the next two weeks visiting cultural sites in the capital city and enjoying local fare under the watchful eye of the Mongolian Prime Minister. Ukweli began to take note of the fact that the prime minister seemed to look for opportunities to speak with Ava alone. During their visit to a local museum, each time Ukweli allowed himself to roam to an art piece that was of interest, he would inevitably look back to find the prime minister in Ava's ear. Ukweli trusted Ava explicitly. Ukweli did not trust the prime minister.

In the hotel, the night before he was to meet the Black Swan, Ukweli asked Ava about her conversations with the prime minister.

"So, what were you and the PM talking about today?"

"When? What do you mean?"

"Come on, Ava. He's been in your ear since we got here. At the museum. At every meal. I'm surprised you heard any of the music at the concert today."

"Ahh, he's a bit of a showoff. He likes everyone to know how much he knows about the art and culture of Mongolia. He was filling me in on the history of each song. He has a real passion for the music of his people."

"Hmm. Is that all he was doing? Filling you in?"

"UK, what are you insinuating?"

"I'm not insinuating anything. I'm just saying that every time I turned around, he was attached to the side of your face. He may as well have been one of your earrings."

"Aww, that's adorable. The mighty Captain Aseyori is jealous!"

"Jealous? Get real. What's there to be jealous about?"

"Well, the prime minister is a very handsome, very rich, very powerful man."

"People like him sit around and dream of living my life."

"Oh, I'm with you, baby. I'm just saying I can see why the Mongolian ladies fall prey to his charms."

"Listen, that being what it is, I don't trust him. I'm grateful for the help he has given us, but I'm starting to wonder when the bill is going to show up. Men like that don't do things like this for free."

"Babe, don't lose sight of why you're here. You can't sit with the guru until you meet with the Black Swan. If the prime minister can expedite that process, then I'll listen to a thousand of his boring stories."

"I'll have to leave you with that clown while I'm in the desert though."

"UK, before I was your wife, I was an agent of the Church. I can handle myself. I'll be fine."

"Yeah, it's not you that I'm worried about."

"Trust me, my love. I'll be counting the breaths until Thysia brings you back to me."

"You'll miss me?"

"I will."

"How much?"

She smiled and reached out her arms toward him, beckoning with her hands. "This much."

JUNE 14, 2045

Kelley sat behind the desk in the executive office of the Church of the Seer. Alexander sat in a chair behind a smaller desk in the west corner. They moved his desk next to the western windows, opposite its original location, because he enjoyed watching the city sunsets. Adam, Paul, Charlotte, and Kei all entered the office together. Adam and Charlotte managed to find air transportation from Egypt just before the sun rose on the seventh. They joined up with Paul and Kei in Barcelona and the four of them managed to fight their way out of Spain. The attacks had been seemingly constant, all torqs but no rogues. The attacks were deliberate and co-ordinated. The group used their guns more than they ever had because of the large number of enemies. They were all surprised to learn that Alexander had been working on his gunmanship in order to help Kelley keep the torqs at bay.

"Kelley is an amazing teacher. I've gotten quite good ac-tually."

"No, he hasn't. But you don't really have to be good to hit a torq when they come in waves. They were sending them to our house in groups of six at first. By the time we called you guys in, they were coming in droves. We were pretty fortunate to make it out the last time."

"We were okay in the bunker in Egypt," Adam said. "It was quite the adventure getting *to* the bunker though."

Paul spoke up. "We did fine in Sapporo. Kei's family was prepared for this type of situation. I'm not exactly sure why." He paused and thought for a few seconds. "Anyway, yeah, we fought off quite a few torqs, but we had plenty of enthusiastic help, so it was never a real burden."

"Heck, maybe we all should've just met up in Sapporo!" Alexander regretted speaking. Kelley took over.

"Okay, at this point, we know that UK and Ava are in Mongolia, but he hasn't started the quest there yet. I'm not sure what the holdup could be, but I know there's a reason. We can only assume, since we're still under such a heavy assault, there is still a possibility for his success. Our job is to stand strong. There's no way UK can do what he needs to do if he's worried about us. We're gonna take the Company's best shot and smile right back at them. If they can't break UK, they sure as hell aren't gonna break us!"

Adam said, "Well, we know they're not gonna attack us here. Do we have any idea how they might come at us?"

Kelley responded, "All we can do is wait. Stay ready. I have a feeling we won't have to wait long."

18

THE MONGOLIAN PRIME MINISTER

JUNE 25, 2045

Ukweli rose at four a.m. on the morning of the drive into the desert. He learned that a walk of gratitude, before sunrise, while things are still cool and quiet, gave the heart enough courage to make it through difficult situations. He didn't know exactly what he was about to face in his encounter with the Black Swan, so a good walk would help him stay focused on the truly important things, namely, rescuing Pax and Kiera from the Dragon.

Ukweli walked around the hotel complex until he located a garden on the grounds. The flowers were aromatic and helped create a sense of calm. The smell vaguely reminded Ukweli of the flower garden at their family estate on Lagos Island. His parents didn't maintain the garden themselves, so they didn't mind when Ukweli and Uzuri played games with their action figures in the garden, occasionally destroying unsuspecting daisies or carnations.

Ukweli sat on the decorative concrete pew, took a deep breath, and began to meditate. His mind created a vision of Uzuri jumping into a swimming pool. He subconsciously smiled. He thought of Kobe and Mara at Christmas in Lagos. He remembered how honored he felt when he saw his team on the ground at the Vatican. He thought of the relief he felt when he and his mates won the Champions League for Tottenham. He thought of his beautiful wife, Ava, and how she cried on his chest as he lay motionless after being pulled from the Caribbean Sea in darkness. Then he thought of Kiera and Pax and his heart became troubled. They were off in a different dimension, held captive by the Dragon, eagerly awaiting someone, anyone, who could come to their aid. Were they safe? Were they being tortured? As Ukweli regained awareness, he was breathing hard and his heart was pounding in his chest. Then he noticed that the sun was coming up. He had been there for over two hours.

Ukweli walked back to the hotel lobby where the prime minister, his executive assistant, and two members of his security detail were waiting. He cordially greeted Ukweli and invited him to his table for breakfast.

"Actually, it's my last morning in town so I'm having breakfast with Ava."

"Oh, no worries. Please join me for a cup of coffee then. I'll brief you on today's activities."

"Sure." The group walked the short distance to the café and took a seat around a large round table.

"Captain, I fear that I haven't been fully transparent with you. I do apologize for that."

"Please, enlighten me."

"You see, I have a great stake in the outcome of your engagement with the Black Swan."

"What kind of stake?"

"While I have no love for Imperium, and certainly the Black Swan has an allegiance to no man, organization, or country, I have been all but assured that you will fail in your quest to retrieve the artifact from the Black Swan."

"In what way does it benefit you for me to fail? You are a very rich and powerful man. You have all that you need."

"I do not have it all. I lack the most primal possession desired by every powerful man; a beautiful woman that is my equal in every way."

"And let me guess, you feel Ava is that woman?"

"Captain, I don't need to tell you that a woman like Ava doesn't grow on buckthorn plants."

"You mean to steal her from me?"

"No, Captain, of course not. I would never disrespect your bond."

"Then you feel she will leave me if I fail?"

"That is where a bit of context might serve you well. You see, Captain, only three in a hundred men who visit the Black Swan survive the trials. Generally, those who do join in service to the Black Swan. Given that you have no intentions of serving his highness, the likelihood of your surviving the trials is practically zero."

"And if I don't survive the trials, you plan on pursuing Ava?"

"Oh no, sir. If you don't survive the trials, Ava has been promised to me as a personal gift from the Black Swan himself. All I have to do is deliver you this afternoon."

"And if she will not have you?"

"I'm sorry for the misunderstanding, but she doesn't have a say in the matter. If you die, she belongs to me."

"Sounds like I had better stay alive then. I'll be down in two hours. Thank you for the coffee."

Ukweli got up and made a brisk but controlled walk to the elevator. He couldn't quite decide how he felt about the prime minister's arrangement with the Black Swan. Had he been disrespected? Is he being set up? He got off the elevator and walked to the room. He paused at the door before he swiped his room key. *What am I supposed to tell Ava?* Just before he swiped his key, Ava opened the door.

"Hey, babe. I ordered breakfast. It should be here any second. You wanna grab a shower before we eat?"

"Yeah, that's great, thanks. Hey, I need to talk to you about something."

"What is it?" Ava asked while she made tea.

"I just talked to the prime minister in the lobby."

"Great. Is everything a go for this afternoon?"

"Yeah, we're all ready to go. Listen, we talked about something else though."

"Really? Something else like what?"

"We talked about you."

"You talked with the prime minister about me?"

"He cut a deal with the Black Swan. If I die doing whatever it is I have to do, the Black Swan has promised the prime minister that he can have you. He would have the rights to you and you would have no say in the matter."

Ava chuckled. "That's just silly locker room talk."

"No . . . no, I don't think it is."

"Ukweli Aseyori, listen to me. The conversation you had with the prime minister this morning was nothing more than a distraction. That's all. They want you to worry about Pax. They want you to worry about Kiera. They want you to worry about me. They want you to think about anything and everything except what you're actually here to do. Well, guess what? I'm not having it. Do you really think I'm vulnerable enough to be used as a pawn in some power-crazy game of desert chess? Please. I *have* a husband, and he happens to be the baddest man on this planet. So don't tell me what will happen if you die. Trust me. Many have tried. All have failed. My man doesn't miss. My man doesn't lose. My man won't be broken. So, if it's all the same to you, I'd appreciate it if you'd hit the shower so you can show me how much you love me before you head into the desert."

Ukweli winked and grinned like a starry-eyed schoolboy. "Yes, ma'am."

Ukweli and Ava walked out of the elevator and into the lobby where they were greeted by the prime minister. Ukweli was adorned in Church of the Seer combat armor, complete with a sword, assault rifles, grenades, and a pistol. Ukweli was sure that the security team surrounding the Black Swan wouldn't allow the weapons, but they needed to know he came prepared for whatever. He also intended to send a powerful message to the prime minister. A warrior in full regalia can be quite intimidating to a debutant-turned-career politician.

"Good afternoon, captain. I hope you and your beautiful wife were able to rest."

"I kept him pretty busy last night . . . and this morning. He may need a nap in the car." Ava smiled, kissed her husband, and turned to walk back toward the elevator.

"Ava," Ukweli called to her as she walked. She hesitated in front of the elevator.

"You got this, right?" She looked annoyed to be forced into the conversation.

"I do." Ukweli smiled.

"Then there's no need for pomp and circumstance. I'll see you when you get back."

Ukweli chuckled. "Yes, ma'am."

"Right this way, captain." The prime minister's security detail pointed the way to the vehicle in the drop-off corridor of the hotel. Ukweli noticed that the prime minister stood still.

"Are you not coming?"

"Oh no. Well, you know, I'm a bit busy here, what, with running the country and all. My people will see to it that you arrive safe and sound in the presence of the Black Swan.

"Of course. Well, thank you for your hospitality. I trust that Ava will be safe here."

"She won't want for a thing. She'll be as safe as if you never left." The prime minister smirked and walked away.

Remington Cross was right. Sometimes regime change is necessary.

Ukweli followed the three security guards and the prime minister's assistant to the vehicle. Ukweli sat in the middle of the back seat, flanked by a guard on each side. There was a guard behind the wheel and the prime minister's assistant sat in the front passenger seat. The group traveled in silence for thirty miles over the rocks into the desert. *This really is a beautiful landscape.* Ukweli marveled at the rock formations before taking a deep breath as the car slowed to a halt.

"Captain Aseyori, I'm afraid this is where your journey ends." The assistant turned around in her seat and faced Ukweli. She spoke with her glasses pulled down on her nose.

"Really, are we there already? I thought the journey was five hours."

"The journey to the Black Swan is five hours. Unfortunately, you won't make it that far."

"You know, the most disappointing thing is that he didn't even send torqs. I really thought he respected me more than this. Anyway, if any of you want to walk away from this, the time is now. On second thought . . ."

Ukweli quickly sent a sharp elbow into the nose of the guard on his right and a powerful right cross to the chin of the guard on his left. He grabbed the necktie of the driver and doubled it around his neck and pulled until it popped. He smashed the face of the guard on the right through the window, shattering the glass. He grabbed a large piece of the broken glass and thrust it into the temple of the guard on the left. He stretched his arms as if he were just awakening from a long night's sleep. The prime minister's assistant sat, shaking and shocked, in the front seat with her mouth open.

"I'm sorry, Miss . . ."

"Mendoza."

"Mendoza? That's not a Mongolian name."

"I'm Filipina." Her voice quivered.

"Ahh, cool, cool. Ms. Mendoza, I suggest you make wiser choices when it comes to your professional circle."

Mendoza tried to regain something that resembled control. "The prime minister will have your head for this."

"See, that's what I mean. If you plan on staying in high-level politics, you need to do a better job of associating yourself with people of character. A single poor choice could cost you everything."

"The prime minister is one of the most powerful—"

"Okay, you're not listening. Things will be a little clearer for you back at the hotel. I don't have time to explain it to you. From me to you, you're very beautiful and you seem smart. Do better." Ukweli opened the door on the left, shoved the body of the guard out onto the ground, and let himself out of the vehicle. "I'm just gonna go in on foot from here if it's all the same to you. Please be careful heading back in. I've been told it can be pretty dangerous."

Ava placed her book on the nightstand and got up to answer the knock at the door.

"Who is it?"

"It's the prime minister, dear." Ava opened the door.

"You have come all alone?"

"Yes. I just wanted to check on you to be sure you have everything you need. I want you to be as comfortable as possible."

"Oh, how thoughtful. I'm fine for now. I'm just eagerly awaiting my husband's return." The prime minister walked into the room and sat on the edge of the bed.

"Oh, dear. About that. I'm afraid I'm the bearer of terrible news. I've just received word that Captain Aseyori and my security team were ambushed as they headed into the desert. The captain fought with great bravery but did not survive. My team barely escaped with their lives."

Ava put her hand to her mouth and began to sob. "Oh no! How could this be?!" She sat beside the prime minister and hugged him. "I'm in need of comfort in my time of such extreme sorrow!" She grabbed the prime minister by the face and kissed him. "Do you think you can provide me with the comfort I so desperately need?!"

"Why, Ava, I will certainly do my very best!" He undid his tie and began to unbutton his shirt.

There was a beep and static from the top drawer in the nightstand.

Ava pulled away from the prime minister. "Excuse me for a moment please." She walked to the drawer and pulled out a small chrome communicator. "Go."

Ukweli spoke from the other end. "It's done. Mendoza is on her way back to you."

"Copy. No distractions. Love you, babe."

"Love you too. Out."

"What? What is this?" The prime minister slid away from Ava but stayed seated on the bed.

"Mr. Prime Minister, this is what we at the Church of the Seer call . . . regime change." Ava retrieved a pistol, equipped with a silencer from the holster under her robe and sent one bullet into the prime minister's forehead, one into his mouth, and one into the center of his chest.

⑲

THE BLACK SWAN

Ukweli walked for three hours over rock and sand and was surprised at how inviting the landscape turned out to be. There was a lot to see and Ukweli took it all in. He decided he would take the opportunity to meditate again. *How often will I ever be able to meditate in a setting like this?* Ukweli sat, lifted his face, and took a deep breath. However, before he could form a thought, a black truck sped to his location. Gun barrels were aimed at his face from behind darkened windows.

"Captain Aseyori, we would be honored if you would come with us. The Black Swan will see you now."

"Thank you, gentlemen."

"Sir, we must request your sword and your firearms."

"Of course."

"And your armor as well please."

"Very well."

Ukweli drew his sword and unbuckled his armor plate.

He reached to his sides and drew his rifles and laid them on the ground beside the armor.

"The handgun as well please, sir."

"I'm getting to it." Ukweli reached to the small of his back and grabbed the pistol and threw it on the ground beside the others.

"Get in."

Ukweli climbed into the passenger seat.

"Put this on." The man seated directly behind Ukweli handed him a burlap sack and instructed him to put it over his head.

They drove for thirty minutes until they came to a large rock formation with a spacious cave between two pillars. The vehicle turned and maneuvered into the cave. The driver turned on the headlights and drove slowly for ten minutes into the depth of the cave, curving and winding until it came to a stop. "Get out. Put your hands behind your back." Ukweli exited the vehicle and raised his hands. One of the men walked behind him and placed the tip of a gun barrel on his back. "Fine. Walk." Ukweli walked about fifty yards, mostly in a straight line. "Get on your knees." Ukweli knelt. "Both knees down." Ukweli put the other knee down. The man removed the bag from his head to reveal a large wood-burning fire pit with a chair on the other side.

"Captain Aseyori, please sit. Relax."

"You're the Black Swan?" Ukweli lowered his hands and sat as he spoke. The Black Swan was an aging Asian man with a long, gray braided beard. He wore a pair of denim jeans and a navy-blue T-shirt with a vintage New England Patriots logo. Ukweli raised an eyebrow.

"I am. Welcome. Your reputation precedes you."

"Likewise. So, you know why I'm here."

"Save the world bit, right? It all seems dramatic to me, but we do what we feel we must."

"How do we proceed?"

"Ahh, you have certainly learned from Cross. Straight to business, huh? Very well. Captain, the whole world will know of your encounter here. Seeing as you have no plans to serve our cause, I cannot allow you to leave without a true test of your character. I will warn you in advance that no man has ever survived the trial you will endure. If you are still alive at sunrise eleven days from now, you will walk away free with the artifact you need. Unfortunately, no one has ever awakened on day four, so you're fighting quite the . . . uphill battle. However, if you happen to live through the trial, you will have earned the respect and favor of the Black Swan forever. Let us feast and toast to the life of Captain Aseyori!" Seemingly all at once, one hundred men dressed in black with covered faces holding swords emerged from the darkness of the caves and shouted, "*Ukhel dekh ner tor! Ukhel dekh ner tor! Ukhel dekh ner tor!*" (Dignity in Death!)

A massive celebration began with beer, wine, and other strong drinks Ukweli didn't recognize. Ukweli didn't drink alcohol very often, so he tried to limit his intake, particularly given his unfamiliarity with some of the drinks, which was difficult with the Black Swan watching his every move. One man handed Ukweli a goblet and shouted, "*Sarlagiin tsus!*" (Yak Blood!) It was warm and thick, and it smelled and tasted disgusting with a metallic finish. Ukweli was sure it was some type of animal blood, and he almost threw up.

The feast consisted of pressed bread with spiced lamb and rabbit cooked over open flames. Ukweli found the food delicious and was genuinely honored by the celebration. *This is as a funeral should be.* The feast lasted until sundown when the men very quickly cleaned and cleared the scene. Twenty men remained visible in the cave along with Ukweli and the Black Swan.

"Now, captain, these are the parameters of your trial. There are four possible outcomes. You may choose not to endure the trial, at which point we will put one hundred arrows into your body and deliver your remains to your wife in the capital city. You may choose to endure the trial and elect at any point in the next eleven days to receive mercy. At that point, we will put one hundred arrows into your body and deliver your remains to your wife in the capital city. You may choose to endure the trial until you expire. At that point, we will honor your sacrifice and deliver your remains, as is, to your wife in the capital city. And, of course, you may choose to endure the trial and endure them successfully. At that point, at sunrise on day eleven, you will be escorted to the hotel with the artifact you seek."

"Let's begin."

"Very well. Your trial is to survive the challenge of the Mongolian adders. These vipers are small in size and, though their venom is extremely painful, it is rarely lethal in small doses." Four men grabbed Ukweli and took him into a dark corner of the cave where he was chained to the wall. The men began to scrub Ukweli with the carcasses of dead mice until his legs were covered with blood and fur.

"Once a viper injects you with venom, it will take about three days to replenish it, so each snake may inject you as many as three or four times in ten days. Only the gods can say for sure how many strikes you will need to endure. You will be provided one meal each day along with water and yak's blood. If you can get it down, the *sarlagiin tsus* can help to fortify your blood's natural defense against the venom, though it has limits in its effectiveness. I do apologize there is no remedy for the pain, though. Good luck, captain. I'll see you in eleven days . . . or sooner."

A man dropped a large canvas bag into the cave and the entrance was covered with a large stone. Day one.

Parishioners at the relatively new Faith Foundation Church in Atlanta filed into service on a bright, sunny Sunday morning. The elders had been leading home groups during the Great Madness, so everyone was excited to return to the in-person service to see the stained-glass windows metamorphose into a kaleidoscope as the sunbeams flooded the sanctuary. Following enthusiastic greetings, everyone participated in the singing of hymns. As the soloist stood for the second verse, there was a loud noise and rumbling in the front lobby.

Suddenly, the doors were flung open, and a large man dressed in red fired a shotgun into the air. Five men, also dressed in all red, followed him into the now-panicked sanctuary. The men closed the rear doors and people started to frantically leave the pews to run to the side doors, only to find them sealed.

"Settle down, everybody. Settle down." A second gunshot. "Settle down before someone gets hurt!" The parishioners stood still, not exactly sure what to do next. "Please, take your seats, I'm just here to talk." Most people slowly moved back toward their seats, though some sat on the floor where they were while others hid under the pews.

"If everyone will just stay calm then nobody will get hurt . . . probably." The men began to walk to the front of the church. "My name is Walker and I'm a representative of the organization known as Imperium, led by Her Majesty,

Jennifer Devore. I'm here on a fact-finding mission. So, the quicker I find my facts, the quicker you good folks can get back to your hypocrisy."

The other men spread out and began to grab adult males from the pews and escorted them to the front. "Now, it has been brought to our attention that several members of this fine congregation have been corresponding with the terrorists from the domestic cell known as the Church of the Seer. While we don't fully understand why you would choose to betray our trust, Jennifer is merciful and has ordered no one be hurt so long as you fully cooperate. That being said, who in this room can tell me how you contact Kelley Jack?" No one moved or spoke. "No worries." Walker turned to the side, cocked his shotgun, and fired a slug into the chest of one of the hostages. Everyone screamed in shock and a few of the older ladies passed out.

"Listen, I'll give you two minutes to discuss it, and then we'll start executing these fine men until you decide to be a little more forthcoming."

"Wait." One of the women in the choir stood up.

"What can you tell me, ma'am?"

"Well, it's just that we don't talk to Kelley Jack or anyone else at the Church of the Seer. They send us encouraging notes from time to time, but they don't actually come here."

"Is that right? They mail these notes to you, like regular snail mail? That's how you get these encouraging notes?"

"Yes, sir. The notes come in the mail like everything else." Walker turned his gun on another hostage, pumped the shotgun, and executed the terrified and confused elder with a single shot.

"We know they've been here. You have two minutes."

Just then, there was an explosion, and the doors at the rear of the sanctuary were blown off the hinges. Kelley Jack stepped just inside the sanctuary.

Walker raised his gun and stepped forward. "Well, speak of the devil. The infamous Kelley Jack has decided to cameo in our production."

"You're going to pay for the lives you've taken here today." Kelley drew her sword. She already had her assault rifle in her left hand. "If you came for me, then come for me. Leave these people alone. I'll be right outside." She turned around and walked through the open doorway. Walker stood in place but ordered the other men to pursue Kelley outside. The men ran in double file down the center aisle and through the doorway only to find Kelley standing in between Charlotte and Kei in the front parking lot. The men engaged the three women but were quickly dispatched by sword and gunfire. Kelley, Charlotte, and Kei moved with precision and intensity before returning to the sanctuary.

Inside, Walker continued to lecture the frightened parishioners.

"I truly hope you understand that Imperium is doing this for you. It was one of the great abolitionists who said, 'I could've rescued many more slaves, had they only known they were slaves.' I'm here to free your minds . . . to open your eyes to the tru—" Just then, Walker was hit in the shoulder with a ninja shuriken and the pain sent him to a knee. He regained his balance and stood only to stare into the silencer-clad barrel of Paul's gun.

"These people have heard enough of your propaganda."

Adam joined Paul at the front and retrieved his throwing star before asking the remaining elders to help remove the bodies from the sanctuary. Walker was taken alive and placed in the back seat of the SUV for interrogation.

"Who are you in Imperium? What is your rank?" Adam asked questions first.

"My name is Walker and I am a centurion. Our task is to

apply pressure to the Church of the Seer by any and all available means."

"If you want to apply pressure to the Church of the Seer, why would you attack and execute innocents?" Though Kelley's rage was apparent, she tried to maintain the appearance of professionalism and control.

"We knew it would draw you into the open. This is just the beginning. These attacks will continue all over the city."

"To what end? It won't stop what UK is doing."

"We can't interfere with the man, but we can keep you busy here. The body count will rise. Attendance will decline. Faith will diminish."

"I will hold you accountable for the lives you have taken today."

Walker began to laugh. "Imagine that. The infamous Kelley Jack. She, with a double-digit body count while practically in diapers, has the audacity to play judge and jury. *You're* going to hold *me* accountable? Look at you. Confident in your righteousness, are you? It doesn't matter how many churches you stroll through or how many Imperium men you add to your mountain of dead bodies, there is no redemption for the Princess of the Church of the Seer. Do what you must, but for every one of us you kill, there will be five more hunting you down. We're here to make your life hell . . . and we're just getting started."

Kelley chuckled. "Walker, Imperium taught you well. But they didn't teach you enough. If you really knew me, you would know that I can't be shamed or intimidated. Send all the torqs you want. Be advised, the more you send, the more that will die by my hands with no hesitation and with no regrets." Kelley retrieved the dagger from beside her thigh and plunged it into Walker's throat. Kelley pulled the blade from the bloody neck, paused for a moment, and proceeded to stab Walker in the chest and abdomen fourteen times, listening for the signature shriek that accompanied the demon escaping the body and dissolving into the air.

The team watched in terror as Kelley executed Walker and were briefly reminded of the darkness in her that gave them pause from the beginning. *That which takes a lifetime to cultivate cannot be easily uprooted.*

Inside the church, the parishioners mourned over the loss of the executed elders and came together to discuss how they would move forward. One of the elders spoke first.

"I would like to say, publicly, how grateful I am for the support of the Seers."

"Support?! Is this what you call support?" A different elder held up his hands as he spoke from the pews. "Our sanctuary decimated. Our leaders executed in front of our children. You heard Walker! They're going to do this all over the city. There's no way the Seers can protect us."

"We must be patient. We must be strong. If we give up now Imperium wins."

"Don't you see it! They've already won! Who will it be next time? You? Me? One of our children? I, for one, don't plan on being a pawn in this war. After all, this building is not the church. *We* are the church. That means the church is wherever we are. Which, from now on, will be in the safety of my living room."

As he got up to leave, one-by-one, parishioners got up from the pews and followed him through what remained of the front door.

Ava sat in the chair beside the desk in her hotel room with her bathrobe covering her clothes underneath. She wore a dark pair of sunglasses that hid her eye movement. Standing over the body of the slain prime minister were Ms. Mendoza, two officers from the Mongolian secret service, a representative from the Mongolian media, the deputy chief of the city police, and a representative from the office of the Mongolian president. The deputy chief looked puzzled as he asked questions.

"So . . . he came to your room and physically assaulted you?"

"Yes."

"So . . . you killed him?"

"Yes."

"And then you called Ms. Mendoza?"

"Yes."

"And, Ms. Mendoza, is this how you remember the events?"

Mendoza looked at Ava. "Yes, detective."

"Is this how the prime minister usually behaves? This seems out of character for the man that I knew."

"You didn't know him as well as I did, detective. He has been known to be aggressive with women and he took a particular liking to Mrs. Aseyori. I heard him remark that she would soon *belong* to him, as if she were an object up for auction."

The president's assistant spoke up. "The president would like to keep this as quiet and as private as possible. No scandals please."

"Hunting accident. Got it." The media representative closed her tablet and left the room.

"Mrs. Aseyori, will you be okay from here?"

"Yes. The hotel has graciously agreed to move my things

to the presidential suite until my husband returns. Thank you so much for your service, detective." Ava and Mendoza walked slowly to the elevator, inserted the room key for the presidential suite, pressed the top button in the elevator, and rode in silence. The elevator doors opened, and Ava swiped the room key at the door. Once inside, Ava turned to Mendoza and smiled.

"Good job, Mendoza."

"As if I had a choice."

"You always have a choice. You made the right one today, sweetie." Ava walked over to Mendoza, turned her around, pulled out a switchblade, and freed Mendoza's hands just before grabbing the grenade that was taped to her, squeezing the trigger, and replacing the pin. "You know, you're free to come to Atlanta with us. There's obviously nothing for you here now."

Mendoza sat at the dining room table, put her face in her hands, and began to cry. "My life. It's ruined. Everything I've worked for. It's . . . gone."

"Oh, please, stop with your sobbing. The prime minister was corrupt and cowardly. That's a recipe for disaster. You're lucky to be alive. I'm offering you a fresh start. You should take it."

"And live the rest of my life in fear? Indebted to a group of international terrorists?"

"If Ukweli wanted you dead, he would've killed you in the desert. He saw potential in you. You can either start from the bottom here in Mongolia with a dark cloud hanging over your head, or you can come with us and make a new start in a new city. At least you won't have to be a boot-licking kiss-ass in Atlanta. You might even find your newfound freedom empowering."

"What am I supposed to tell my family? I'm just up and moving to the United States?"

"Who cares? How about you grow a pair and do what's best for you? It's like you don't trust me at all."

"You killed my boss and taped a grenade to my hands."

"For your own good. Do what you like though. I'm gonna take a bath. If you're still here when I get out, I'll know I have a colleague. Otherwise, good luck."

Ava disappeared behind the large double doors that led to the master bedroom. Mendoza stood up, walked to the couch in the common area, kicked off her high heels, and lay down to take a nap. Before she dozed off, she pulled out her phone and googled *Things to do in Atlanta.*

The pain associated with the snake bites was unlike any physical pain Ukweli had experienced before. The toxin affected the nerves so, while the bites themselves were sharp, the pain traveled up the nerves of the legs and into the back so it felt like a scalpel working its way up from Ukweli's calf to his waist.

Ukweli was sure he would eventually get used to the pain, but the nerve damage that accompanied the swelling made his legs feel like they were on fire and about to burst from the accumulated pressure. Each morning, a group of men entered the room and removed the snakes, followed by a group of women who would come in and give Ukweli a bath and a meal. Ukweli appreciated the bath because he wasn't allowed to be free from the chains to relieve himself. He was very grateful for the women, at least at first. They played a very important and very difficult role. His meal generally consisted of wild desert game cooked in a stew, served with bread and a small vessel of water. The women tried to force-feed him the *sarlagiin tsus*, but the warmth and viscosity made it arduous for Ukweli to fully ingest the metallic, fermented sludge. At least, that was, until day four, when the skin on Ukweli's shins began to split at the bite sites from the swelling, and open wounds began to form. The women did what they could to treat the sites but weren't allowed to bandage open sores. Day five brought labored breathing and an irregular heartbeat. By day six, Ukweli was in and out of consciousness during the day and completely incoherent at night. He no longer felt the fangs break the skin at all, only the surge of pain from the venom. He was just over halfway through the process and his entire existence was relegated to fighting to stay alert enough at night to keep the snakes away from his abdomen, chest, and neck. By day seven, he began to crave the *sarlagiin tsus*, which he convinced himself was coating his insides and easing some of the pain. It was also on day seven that the women began to take advantage of him. The harem began coming in larger groups, three at the beginning, eight by day seven, and smearing his thighs and hips with a compound to increase blood flow to his groin area so they could rape him during the treatment sessions. Ukweli would often pass out during the violations because of the pain, the lack of oxygen from his labored breathing, and the inefficient blood flow. On day eight and day nine, he passed out with one of the women on him and regained consciousness with another having her way. His skin was beginning to turn pale due to the loss of blood as the wounds on his legs refused to close because of the nightly dosage of venom. The women were oppressed under the rule of the Black Swan, so they took the opportunity on day ten to cause physical suffering for Ukweli, a reparation of sorts, by beating him with sticks and small rocks on his arms and chest. They would scream *Shudarga!* (Justice!) before pounding his body. They did not break the skin, but they created several bruised areas on his upper body that further complicated his already troubled breathing.

Ukweli woke up on the afternoon of day eleven to the shock of excruciating pain, as he was being given a saltwater bath to sterilize his wounds before they were wrapped. Shortly thereafter, he laid calmly on a soft mattress, free of chains, the wounds on his legs bandaged, and being fed two bags of electrolyte fluids intravenously.

"Amazing. Absolutely amazing. The mighty captain lives." Ukweli knew that it was the Black Swan speaking, but he couldn't manage to focus his eyes on the source of the sound. The swelling, dehydration, and all manners of abuse also prevented him from being able to speak. "I would like to apologize for the behavior of the girls. They found you so appealing that when your upper body began to swell after a week, we thought you were as good as dead, so I let them have their way with you. I would never have allowed such atrocities had we considered survival a possibility. You'll certainly want to get access to antivenom as soon as you can and, if I were you, probably an antibacterial cocktail as well. I mean it when I say they were not kind to you, sir. I hope your lovely wife will understand."

Not likely, Ukweli thought.

The Black Swan stood and walked over to Ukweli, placed a small vile in his hand, and closed his fingers around it. "You have my respect. Go in peace." Ukweli was placed on a stretcher and loaded into the rear of an antiquated medical transport.

JULY 5, 2045

Ava sat on a grassy area in the flower garden at the hotel and meditated. She was experiencing a high level of anxiety as she expected Ukweli's visit with the Black Swan to last a week or so. After she didn't hear from him on day eight, she began using ashwagandha and valerian to calm her nerves and maintain her resolve. Mendoza hired a Tuvan throat singer to serenade Ava as she rested to further calm her spirit. Ava found it truly bizarre but oddly soothing. As Ava sat in the grass on the warm evening of day eleven, she was interrupted by a frantic hotel attendant.

"Mrs. Aseyori, the transport has arrived with the captain."

Ava stood slowly. She didn't want to admit that a small part of her expected them to return with her husband in a body bag. "How is he?"

"He is alive, but he has suffered greatly. The medical personnel can't say for sure what they have done to him. You should come quickly."

Ava ran to the front of the hotel where they had already unloaded Ukweli. He was on the stretcher, almost completely covered in bandages, and Ava could tell that he was suffering from severe edema. She resisted the urge to throw herself onto him as she could tell he was in great pain.

"Take him upstairs, quickly please." The emergency workers loaded the stretcher onto the elevator and followed Ava's instructions. Mendoza held the front door and the crew quickly moved Ukweli into the living room of the spacious suite. "Remove the bandages on his legs. I need to know what they've done to him."

Ukweli groaned in pain as the workers gently removed the bandages to reveal the open wounds on his legs, some of which continued to degenerate, saturated with venom. Mendoza put her hand to her mouth, partly in shock and disgust, mostly to prevent herself from vomiting.

"I need the antivenom, now! Brown leather bag, yellow bottle. Hurry!"

Mendoza ran into the bedroom and looked in the brown leather bag at the foot of the bed. There was an array of rare emergency medical supplies organized by color, a knife in a sheath, two handguns, two passports, and five stacks of bound cash, each labeled $20,000. She grabbed the small yellow bottle and ran with it into the common area.

Ava took the bottle and loaded a small amount in a syringe. She leaned down and kissed Ukweli, rubbed his forehead, and whispered, "This is gonna hurt, love." She jabbed the needle into the largest of the open wounds as Ukweli squirmed and moaned. Ava barked orders to the medical staff. "Wash him carefully and take care to count the bite marks."

"Bite marks?" Mendoza looked confused. "What did they do to him?"

"These are snake bites. We will need to do a fluid exchange. He is full of venom."

"That's impossible. There must be thirty marks there. There's no way he could survive that."

"Most men couldn't. Mine is different."

"Different how?"

"He's uniquely gifted to endure suffering."

20

THE DRAGON REIGNS

Kiera woke up from a sound sleep and looked around without moving her head. She was in sleeping quarters she didn't recognize, and life had taught her to observe before you move. She didn't notice anyone else in the room, so she sat up on the edge of the bed and stretched her arms a bit. As she looked around, she assumed she was in a hotel room. She stood up to check the area and was relieved there was a restroom. She slowly and carefully sat on the toilet, while remaining focused on her surroundings. As she sat, a female voice came over the speaker in the ceiling.

"Good morning, Mrs. Connaught. I hope you were able to rest."

"My name is Kiera Michaels. And yes, I slept, thank you."

"I apologize. DayStar instructed the staff to refer to you as Mrs. Connaught and that we are to care for your each and every need. But if you would rather be called

Ms. Michaels, we will certainly oblige. DayStar may not be pleased with your decision though."

"I'm not too concerned with what pleases DayStar at the moment, thank you. Where is my son?"

"Oh, of course. He is with DayStar. They are just about to be served breakfast if you would like to join them."

"Sure. I'll need to shower."

"The closet has been fitted with clothes for you and there are toiletries in the drawers. I'll tell him you're coming."

Kiera showered and stood in front of the closet. The doors were fitted with mirrors, and she looked at herself, wrapped in bath towels. *How did it all come to this?* She slid the door open and was pleasantly surprised at the wardrobe that had been assembled on her behalf. *Somebody around here has good taste.* She looked through the lovely clothes but, in the end, opted for comfort and functionality. She chose black yoga pants, a T-shirt with a gray pullover, and black combat boots. They were light but sturdy, just in case she needed to kick somebody. She got dressed, put her hair in a bun, and walked toward the door. When she pulled on the handle the door didn't open.

"Ahh, excuse me, lady in the ceiling? I can't get out."

"I apologize, Ms. Michaels. There is an attendant on the way. He will escort you to breakfast."

At that time, there was a knock on the door and a young man entered the room.

"Ms. Michaels, I'm Tom. I'm here to take you upstairs for breakfast."

"Good morning, Tom. You look young to be working here."

"I'm sixteen, ma'am."

Kiera asked probing questions as they walked to the elevator. "How is it that you have managed to end up . . . wherever it is we are?"

"I was created here . . . for the service of DayStar, ma'am."

"You were created? Do you have parents?"

"Parents? No. No, ma'am. No parents, ma'am. I'm only here for service."

They arrived at the elevator and Tom placed his hand on the doors at the connection point. The doors opened and the two of them stepped inside. The doors slowly closed and immediately opened again to reveal a lush green garden filled with flowers and plants of all varieties and colors sitting adjacent to a calm flowing stream. Kiera was escorted to a large gazebo set up as a breakfast nook. There she saw Jackson, dressed in a red suit, sitting at a table, with Pax in a highchair seated near him. There were two men in red suits standing behind Jackson and there were two women in red dresses seated on either side of Pax. Pax was dressed in a red onesie with the words, "Mama's Boy" on it. He was content with a red binky in his mouth.

"Good morning, Kiera. I'm so glad you decided to join us for breakfast."

"Jackson, where the hell are we?"

"Interesting choice of words. We're not in hell, per se. But you can think of it as hell adjacent."

"Hell adjacent?"

"Sure. You know how if you go to a conference at a large hotel, like the Connaught, the guest rooms are in one section of the facility, while the conference rooms are adjacent?"

"Yes."

"It's kind of like that. We're not in kolasi, but we are in an adjacent dimension."

"Adjacent dimension? This is all just too much."

"This is my home of sorts. The Dragon dimension was constructed for me. It's where I draw strength. I'm in complete control here."

"That doesn't explain why I'm here. It doesn't explain why Pax is here."

"Well, that's not what you asked. You only asked where we were, not why."

"Dammit, Jackson, what the hell is going on?"

"Wow, language . . . do you kiss your mother with that mouth? And in front of Pax no less. I guess that's just how you were raised."

"You control a hell-adjacent dimension and you're judging me?"

"Fair point. Listen, have a seat, enjoy your breakfast, and I'll explain everything while you eat."

"Fine. What are we having?"

"Well, I remembered you liked egg-white omelets."

"Yeah, when I was playing soccer. You think I'm gonna sit in hell and eat egg whites?"

"Hell-adjacent. Okay, so no egg whites. Look, just walk over and tell the chef what you want. He can make anything."

Kiera walked over to the chef and requested an acai bowl with tropical fruit and *pão de queijo*. She walked back to the table and picked up Pax and sat back down.

"Okay, Mr. DayStar, sir. Start talking. Why are we here?"

"You're here because Pax is here. Pax is here because I had to keep him away from his father."

"We're here because you don't want me to be with Ukweli?"

"See? That right there. That's why our marriage was doomed. You think you know everything, and you don't listen."

"Geez, sorry."

"I don't have to keep you away from UK. He's married, in case you forgot. And he and his darling wife are closer than ever. So, for however much you think he loves you, he made his choice, and it wasn't you. It's never been you. He moved on. Maybe you should do the same. But I digress. I didn't say I needed to keep *you* away from UK. I said I needed to keep *Pax* away from him. As fate would have it, Pax is the only thing standing between me and total conquest. Since the Magician won't allow me to—eh 'hem—*discard* . . . of Pax, I just need to keep him away from UK until I can figure out what to do next."

"So, you're just gonna hide out here forever?"

"Again, you speak words of irony. It seems that your dysfunctional family reunion will happen sooner than we thought."

"What does that mean, Jackson?"

"It means that UK has shown himself capable and he is very close to acquiring the means to visit us here. It seems he's coming for Pax."

"He's coming for me too, Jackson."

"You're delusional." Jackson's facial expression was one of frustration, disbelief, and amusement.

"Whatever."

"He's coming for Pax. He'll be here soon."

"Ahh, I see. You're afraid."

"I've never been afraid of UK. He's never bested me in a single competition."

"He bested you in the only competition that ever mattered to you. He won my heart."

"You flatter yourself. Had I known you were the strumpet you've turned out to be, I never would have pursued you in the first place. I have no care for you or this bastard child, aside from how I can destroy you both and claim my throne. If you continue to test my patience, you'll learn for yourself the kind of power I truly have here."

"Ukweli is on his way and he's gonna kick your ass when he gets here."

"Bitch, please. Take your plate to go."

"I'm not leaving without Pax."

"Kiera, you're in the Dragon dimension. You're my prisoner here. You have no authority. You're not calling the shots. Plus, you have no resources. You don't have diapers or food. Pax is being cared for. So, please, just go."

"Jackson . . ."

"Tell your story walking."

The Great Eternal Paradox – Issue 4, July 9, 2045

Apology plus Preparation

Please accept our sincere apology for the uptick in Company oppression. It's not about you. Unless, of course, it is. The Company wants you afraid. They want you distracted. They want you to abandon your mission and dilute your efforts. You are the modern-day Hebrews. Don't allow the persecution to draw you away from following the example of Thysia! The only way they win is for you to stop. Stop giving to the poor. Stop encouraging one another. Stop thinking of others. That's how they win. You may have to take some unprecedented steps to protect yourselves. You may have to arm your capable parishioners. You may have to fight! So be it! What on earth is worth protecting more than the bride of the sacrifice?

JULY 12, 2045

Ukweli opened his eyes slowly and allowed them to adjust to the uncomfortable light. His eyes burned as he looked around to try to assess his whereabouts. He realized he was on a mattress, but he didn't recognize the room. Ava walked in and noticed he was awake.

"Hey, babe. How are you feeling?" She sat on the bed beside him.

"My eyes are burning."

"You've been out for a few days. We had to do a fluid replacement. Your body was saturated with venom."

"The vipers."

"You had forty-nine snake bites on your legs and abdomen. I had to use both vials of antivenom."

"You saved my life again."

"Yeah, I love you too."

"My body is hurting. I feel like I have the flu."

"You should be so lucky. There was extensive bruising on your chest and arms. They started beating you at some point. They didn't break the skin, but you'll be sore for a while."

"No worries."

"Some worries."

"Huh?"

"There is quite a bit of chaffing on your groin area."

"My groin area?"

"Your penis, UK. There is severe chaffing on your penis."

"Yeah," Ukweli sighed.

"Yeah, what?" Ava was noticeably agitated and made more so by Ukweli's apparent lack of concern.

"They took advantage of me."

"What does that mean, UK? What did they do?"

"Yeah . . . they raped me."

"Who raped you?"

"The women. Initially, they came in to care for me, but their motivations changed."

"You must've enjoyed it on some level. You had to have

been aroused." Ava spoke with her arms crossed and her head slightly leaning to the side. In that moment, she was equal portions jealous, angry, and worried. A small part of her was tempted to threaten Ukweli with her blade.

"They massaged me with some kind of compound to create an erection."

"What?! How many . . . women? How many women were there?"

"I don't know. It was the last few days of the trial and I always passed out during."

Ava stood silently and processed the new information. Ukweli was distracted by the pain and couldn't tell what she was thinking. The lights pierced his eyes, so he found it easier to just keep them closed.

"Okay. Hey, I'll be back."

"Wait, where are you going?"

"You won't be ready to travel for another few days but, unfortunately, we don't have time to waste. We'll leave for Gasherbrum tomorrow morning, so you need to rest."

"Wait, I need you here."

"You'll be fine. Mendoza is here if you need anything."

Ukweli was slightly startled when he woke up to find Mendoza sitting in the chair next to the bed. There was a beige tray with a plate of pasta with red sauce and two dinner rolls on the stand near his head.

"You hungry?"

Ukweli suspiciously looked around the room. "Uh, what's up Mendoza? Where is Ava?"

"I don't know. She said she would be back by sunrise, but she didn't tell me where she was going."

"What time is it?"

"It's almost eleven. Are you hungry?"

"I am but that marinara is gonna make me throw up."

"You want me to find you something else?"

"I think I'll be fine until morning."

"You know you have to eat if you're going to recover. Ava won't be happy I couldn't get you to."

"Ava will be fine. Why are you all dressed up?" Ukweli sat up on his elbows.

"Cabin fever. I'm going down to the bar for a drink."

"Wait. You're just gonna leave me here?"

Mendoza stood up from the chair and slowly walked to the edge of the bed and sat down facing Ukweli. She wore a form-fitting white dress with green lace-up high heel sandals, and she carried a small green, cross-grain leather clutch in her right hand. Her naturally black hair had been dyed blond for about a week and was being held back by a green tie-back headband. She switched the purse to her left hand and placed her right hand on Ukweli's chest.

"Well, captain, Ava did say I should take care of you while she was gone. Is there anything I can help you with right now?"

Ava returned to the hotel the following morning and brought Ukweli a cup of warm chicken broth and a small bowl of assorted crackers.

"Good morning, babe. You need to try to eat something before we get going."

"Ava, where have you been?"

"I had business to handle, UK. Mendoza said you haven't eaten. Here, see if you can stomach this."

"What kind of business? Ava, what did you do?"

"I closed the account with the Black Swan."

"Closed the acc—Ava . . . what, exactly, did you do?"

"The Black Swan is no longer an ally."

"Ava . . ."

"He allowed his servants to act outside of the parameters of the trial. I let him live but your harem was not as fortunate."

"Wait, you killed the women?"

"Yes."

"All of them?"

"Yes."

"How many women did you kill, Ava?"

"Eight."

Ukweli slouched his head to the side to express his frustration. "Woman, you must work on that temper."

"I'm not emotional or temperamental. You have things to do and I'm here to support you. I understand you must do these things alone. However, if someone takes advantage of you, I take that personally and I will not let it stand. The world will know to think twice."

"My wife . . ."

"Let's get you fed and loaded up. We're flying into Islamabad. Plane leaves in two hours."

Ukweli relaxed his head on a pillow and tried to disguise the uneasiness brewing in his gut. Ava initially joined the Church of the Seer to serve. She was a healer at heart and desired to be a part of a global movement. Remington Cross paired Ava with Ukweli because of her staunch loyalty. Cross expressed concern that Ukweli lacked resolve and he hoped Ava's influence would keep the captain focused. While Cross fully anticipated and embraced the darkness that developed in Ukweli, he always hoped Ava could provide him with the balance necessary to function away from the sword.

By the time the couple left Rome, however, Ava had become so enamored with Ukweli that rather than leading him toward the light, she began to follow him down the path of unrighteousness. First, she learned to kill, then she learned to enjoy killing. Now, it seemed that, even though she was a highly trained medic, she was losing the basic appreciation for human life. Though Ukweli could see what she was becoming, and he regretted his role in it, he appreciated who Ava was. He, in fact, needed her to be that right now. Besides, he couldn't exactly pour into her what he himself lacked.

JULY 29, 2045

Kelley and Alexander sat in their living room in Atlanta, enjoying the latest episode of *Vine City Shawties*. Alexander relaxed in the recliner under a heated blanket. Even though it was the middle of summer, he was always cold. Kelley sat on the couch on the seat farthest to the right, the closest seat to Alexander.

Kelley often chuckled at the thought of falling in love with a man as corny as him. He was everything she wasn't; innocent, compassionate, funny, and he was far more of a girl than she had ever been allowed to be. Maybe her connection to him was an attempt to capture some resemblance of childhood purity. Kelley had never been given that option. Her life had been about survival since she was found in a dumpster as a newborn.

"I don't know why you insist on watching this show, Alex. It's dramatic for no reason."

"I watch for the shawties. They're from the mean streets, yet they've managed to make a path to respectability."

"See? That's what I'm talking about though. First of all, who even says shawties? Literally no one. And trust me, I know what it's like to live on the *mean streets*. Vine City ain't it. That's one thing I'll give Jackson credit for. He really cleaned up that whole area during his stint as mayor. With super selfish motives, of course, but still."

"Kelley, you spent your formative years in a monastery just like I did. Is that what you're calling the mean streets?"

"I was in a monastery, but it wasn't like yours. A priest taught me how to fight and use weapons so I could protect myself from the other men who tried, daily, to take advantage of me. You're a grown man and you still can't fight or shoot."

"Well, let's just be thankful I have you for all of that."

"Wow. I know they say opposites attract, but c'mon, there is no formula that can describe us."

"What do you mean? There's nothing complicated or odd about us. You simply couldn't resist my masculine wiles."

"As you sit under a blanket eating white cheddar popcorn." Kelley noticed as Alexander snuggled under the warm blanket, pulling it up just under his chin.

"Yes. As we speak, my charms are mesmerizing." Alexander made a flowing movement with his hands. Kelley laughed. She hopped off the couch and lifted the blanket and made room for herself on his lap. She sat down and rested her head on his shoulder.

"This war is exhausting."

"Certainly, you must grow weary from the killing."

"No, that's actually the best part."

"The killing is the best part, Kelley?"

"Yes. They deserve to die. I feel as though I owe it to them."

"Please remember that vengeance belongs to Thysia."

"Then I am his chosen vessel. It is my great honor to exact his vengeance. I'm just getting tired of defending people who no longer trust us."

"Kelley, you're not called into vengeance. You're called to defend the Bride."

Kelley lifted her head and gave Alexander a puzzled look. "Here you go with that again. I admit that Thysia showed up in Rome in a mighty way. But where is he now, Alex? Imperium is executing citizens every week and we're the only ones doing anything about it! Plus, we still don't know where they'll show up tomorrow. I guess it's a good thing the churches are mostly empty these days."

"Thysia has protected us in ways we don't even know about. And we all know there's no way UK could do what he's doing without Thysia. As long as Imperium controls the government, we remain Thysia's hands and feet. Don't grow weary in well doing."

"I know, I know. I've just never seen so many torqs. They're coming at us in waves. I'm excited and disgusted. I'm starting to smell like them."

"You smell perfectly divine to me." They kissed and she returned her head to his shoulder and drifted off to sleep.

(21)

PAKISTAN

AUGUST 1, 2045

Ukweli rose early for his morning run. He decided to let Ava sleep in. She had given so much and her activities in Mongolia took a toll on her, even if only subconsciously. *She takes such good care of me.* As he ran, Ukweli began to think of the times Ava not only cared for him, but literally saved his life. She even helped save Kiera and Pax in Rome. *Where would I be without her?*

Ukweli thought about Pax every day. Of course, it was impossible to think about Pax without thinking about Kiera. Everything he was doing, everything he was going through, was so he could get to them. *Pax is the key to saving the world.* Ukweli didn't understand it and, honestly, he wasn't motivated to save the world. He was motivated to save Pax . . . and Kiera.

Could he honestly be in love with Kiera, knowing everything he now knew about Ava? *We've been through so much together. Is Kiera just a distraction?* DuaTre referred to Kiera as Ukweli's "light." *What did she mean by that?* Ava had proven her loyalty to the point that not only could Ukweli see a future with her, but he struggled to see a future without her. How would this all end? Ukweli was glad he didn't have to make that decision today.

He felt the strength returning to his legs as he ran. There was still a great deal of pain present, but the wounds had begun to heal, and his stamina was returning. He knew his friends were suffering in the meantime, but Gasherbrum is known as the Hidden Peak because of its remoteness, and the climb would be a test of endurance. He simply couldn't afford to go before his body showed signs of recovery. Again, he had Ava to thank for that. Her quick thinking and level of preparedness made it all possible. *Who travels with antivenom anyway?* As it turns out, what Ukweli thought was a normal leather tote was actually a "keep Ukweli alive" duffel. Just another reason he loved her.

Ukweli decided to push his body this morning. He ran toward the foothills and did some intermediate sprint work on the inclines. His lungs burned as he pulled the small hills and he found it invigorating. He had to reteach his body how to respond to the extreme demands of the climb ahead. Each trial offered a unique challenge and his trek to the guru would rival the others. It wasn't that the climb would be a death-defying feat, Gasherbrum isn't one of the ten highest peaks, but making the climb alone would offer pitfalls that would be far simpler for a team. The thought made Ukweli think of Adam and Paul and, for a brief moment, he wished they were going with him.

When Ukweli returned to the cabin, Ava was sitting on the couch in the front room sipping from a smokey cup of tea. She prepared a smoothie with protein powder, fruit, hemp milk, and ice for Ukweli and he found it to be nourishing and refreshing. *What doesn't she do perfectly?*

"Thank you for breakfast."

"How was your run?"

"It felt good to be able to push myself again. I think I'm almost ready."

"That's good. Because it's time. I know we can't send you up that mountain before you're ready, but I can't help but think of our friends. They're counting on us."

"Yeah, I know. I can admit I've dreaded this. I have no idea what the guru is going to tell me. What if he doesn't accept the artifacts? What if it turns out he's just some crazy old loon? What if I get there and he's frozen in the snow?"

"Ukweli Aseyori, now you listen to me. Given what we've seen over the past few months, can you really dread anything? Thysia has a hedge around you even I don't fully understand. You've survived being at the bottom of the ocean for hours and having your body pumped full of snake venom. Not to mention whatever happened in Rome. With everything you've experienced, all the torqs you've faced, the governments you've toppled, the impossible tasks . . . are you still questioning yourself?"

"No, I'm not questioning myself. Sometimes I do wonder when my luck might run out though."

"There's a big difference between luck and destiny."

Ukweli loved it when Ava used her words to motivate him. She was good at reminding him who he was. She consistently spoke strength and power into him, and it always made him feel like he could do anything. He finished the last cool swallow of his breakfast and turned to look at his wife. She was in a tank and shorts and her enhancement-free face was brown and soft. Her coarse, black hair was pulled into a ponytail.

Ava sat her teacup down and picked up her book. He watched her fingers as she turned the pages, and it nearly sent him into a frenzy. He put his mug on the table and started walking toward her. She glanced up and immediately recognized the look in his eyes. She allowed the book to rest on her legs and she used both hands to point to the back of the suite.

"Hey . . . shower first." He smiled and moved briskly toward the bathroom, his steps spritely with anticipation.

AUGUST 3, 2045

Ukweli stood outside in the surprisingly green grass at the base camp. He had climbed before, but never alone, and the jagged peaks and sheer faces of Gasherbrum loomed beckoning, taunting. Ascending in solitude to convene with Bing Ren promised to be the challenge of a lifetime, but there was something invigorating about the frigid air and Ukweli knew he was closer to Pax right now than he had been since the trials began. That thought alone was enough to get him up and going. He didn't even need his usual pep talk from Ava. He left her in bed. He knew she would be pleased to wake up and find him gone. She was.

Ukweli had the proper gear for the climb, but he learned it wasn't the gear that kept you alive. In addition to gear, a successful climber needs physical strength, stamina, heart, instincts, and motivation. All climbers consider quitting before reaching the summit. It takes mental toughness and self-awareness to see it through.

Ukweli started up the rocky bottom, which quickly inclined. At a certain grade, climbs begin to feel like ladders, as if you're walking straight up into the clouds. Peering through his goggles, he could see the path before him and, even as his legs started to burn, he felt himself gaining energy. The wounds from the vipers in the desert healed well. He had Ava to thank for that. There was something about surviving the Gobi trials that made him feel even more prepared for the climb. It was as if the surge of snake venom had given him supernatural abilities. Maybe he could be a new superhero. SnakeMan didn't really sound like a character kids could get behind, but they loved heroes based on spiders and bats, so who's to say they wouldn't eventually embrace SnakeMan too?

He smiled as he rhythmically walked, step by step, up the curvy trail. It was very early in the trip on the first day he encountered the jaguar. Ukweli stopped and stood still as the creature made its way down a side hill to stand directly in the path in front of Ukweli. He had never seen an actual jaguar in the wild, but he had encountered lions in Africa and tigers in Asia, and he was genuinely shocked at the sheer size of the creature. Its fur was thick and shimmering white. It had black feet and piercing blue eyes. White jaguars were considered folk tales and had never been seen in the wild. Of course, anyone who encountered a creature this size would likely not live to tell about it anyway. As it grew closer, Ukweli could see that it was much larger than the largest of the tigers he saw in Tibet.

There was no way to escape and Ukweli didn't want to rouse the creature by reaching for his sword. He reached to his thigh to clutch his dagger and felt silly even holding it in his hand. His heart rate began to rise, and he felt his breathing become labored. *Focus. Thysia didn't bring you all this way to die here.* He replaced the dagger and walked toward the creature. He stopped for a moment when the creature made a sudden move toward Ukweli, lifted its large head, and let out a roar that shook the rocks and ice. The jaguar looked at Ukweli, then the path, then Ukweli again.

Ukweli nodded respectfully and turned from the large, wide path to the far narrower path that brought the jaguar down the mountain. The beast quietly followed.

The path was rocky and steep and required more climbing than walking. The sheer, flinty walls were covered with clear ice and a vacuum created a continuous flow of frigid air. Ukweli smiled as he thought about the physical challenge ahead of him. His legs were already beginning to burn from the climbing, and it made him happy. His happiness was short-lived, however, as he remembered he was being followed by a twelve-hundred-pound natural hunter that just as accurately could have been described as stalking him. He consciously kept his steps sure and consistent so as not to give the jaguar a reason to think he was giving up, perhaps providing the beast with an easy meal.

Ukweli trekked what was noticeably becoming an upward spiral for nine hours. The more he climbed, the colder and stronger the icy wind blasts became. Ukweli paused for a moment, needing a respite from the narrowing of the pathways in his lungs, but was quickly reminded by the deep bass in the growl of the beast that he should proceed.

So, he did.

Ukweli climbed, higher and higher, until the sunlight dissipated. He wasn't entirely sure when, but the beast, once behind him, now walked beside him. Ukweli likely wouldn't have noticed the jaguar's change in position in the dark, but the beast was now starting to nudge Ukweli toward the left into an open space. Ukweli walked into the space and was relieved to find there was no airflow. It was very cold and very dark in the cave and Ukweli assumed the beast led him to the spot to camp for the night. He was, at least, partially correct.

Ukweli removed his backpack and sat it on the ground.

He quickly grabbed two pieces of lamb jerky from the side pouch and shoved one piece into his mouth and the other into his pocket. He turned the bag to the other side and removed the canteen. He then reached for the top zipper on the pack but was abruptly interrupted by the beast as it used a sweeping motion with a massive paw to quickly move the pack away from Ukweli's reach. Ukweli would not be allowed to use his tent or any of his other supplies as they rested just ten feet away, under the loving care of the creature.

Even when Ukweli used the climbing rope attached to a hook on his waist to create a makeshift bed (it created a much-needed buffer between him and the icy cave floor) the beast violently snatched the rope from under Ukweli, causing him to roll several feet, crashing to an awkward landing before sliding a few extra feet on the ice. It became clear to Ukweli that part of the trial to be deemed worthy of an audience with Bing Ren was surviving the night in the cave. No tent. Just ice. The temperature held steady at a mild fifteen degrees below zero.

(22)

INHABITATION

Ann Jefferson and Jennifer Devore sat at the round table by the clear spring enjoying a French brunch consisting of croque monsieurs, omelets with caviar, and white chocolate croissants with mimosas made with freshly squeezed juice.

"What a beautiful atmosphere you've created for yourself here."

Jackson lifted a single eyebrow. "Yeah, thanks. Why are you guys here again?"

"We wanted to see if you needed anything," Ann spoke with a full bite of croissant in her mouth. "We know the man will be here soon. We wanted to be sure you were ready."

"Of course I'm ready. What do you think I've been doing here?"

"Well, we know the girl has rejected you again. The disappointment of rejection can often cause one to lose their resolve." Jennifer took small, elegant bites that showed her teeth.

"Kiera didn't reject me."

"She loves the man and carried the child. Though it was ordained, we understand it feels like rejection." Ann, again, spoke muffled words, blanketed this time by ham and cheese.

"Listen, you two, UK is on his way here. Can you please be useful in some way?"

"Of course. We have good news. We have been given clearance to launch a full-scale assault."

"But my father said the Beautiful One gave instructions that lent toward subtlety."

"Until he saw our latest results."

"What results?"

"Our task units have been assassinating random church goers on Sunday mornings."

"Have the Seers not responded?"

"Of course. They have killed hundreds."

"Then what good news do you have?"

"The churches are nearly empty now. They do not trust the Seers to protect them, and they lack the strength to protect themselves. They have begun to succumb to the fear."

"How does this help me?"

"You will learn to consume the fear. Plus, it may be that, by the time the man arrives, his world will be in such disarray, he will be weakened by grief and discouragement."

"I don't need help defeating UK. I've beaten him before, and I'll do it again. I only need *YOUR* help if *HE* gets help."

Jennifer spoke soberly. "If the Magician intervenes, the Beautiful One only expects you to fight valiantly."

"Wait . . . what? What do you mean, fight valiantly? The last time he showed up, a four-story-tall angel grabbed me in his hand and dragged me to hell. And you're telling me to fight valiantly?"

"Yes, fight valiantly."

"Okay, so you guys are afraid of him."
Jennifer and Ann disappeared.

"It's time for a national divorce. The accountability began in the churches in my capital city of Atlanta but has since spread all over the country and into South America. We're so fortunate that Imperium is here to protect us from the evil of the Seers. Imperium and the Company have the full support of the state of Georgia as they continue to expose and dispose of the opposition while hunting down the traitors. As the Movement continues to spread worldwide, I request that Imperium be given the complete support of the US government. We should provide necessary aid as our allies hunt down the terrorists from the Church of the Seer and punish all who show loyalty to their anti-American causes!"

—Excerpt from a speech given on the floor of the US Congress by Representative Randall Frederick Moore of Georgia

AUGUST 4, 2045

"Hello."
"Hi, Paul, it's Alexander."
"Yeah, hey, buddy. You and Kelley okay?"
"No."
"Are you being attacked?"
"No."
"Alexander, what's the problem?"

"It's Kelley. I'm afraid she's gone mad."

"Uhh, Alex, buddy, you knew Kelley was loco when you decided to be with her."

"Paul, I've seen such a change in her. Underneath that stony exterior beats a heart of gold and her encounter with Thysia exposed it. But now . . ."

"But now what?"

"Kelley's out in the city right now."

"What?! She knows it's too dangerous to be out alone! She gave us squatting orders herself!"

"She goes out into the city *because* it's dangerous."

"I don't understand."

"She has once again grown to love killing. All she ever talks about is killing. She's written poetry inspired by the sound of the demons escaping a dying host. *My sword, my steel, strong and cold; I pierce your flesh, you screech and hiss; Before the story, completely told; The body drops, dissolves to mist.* Paul, even when we—well—when we . . . you know . . ."

"Goodness, Alexander. You're not thirteen. You have sex."

"Yes, when we have sex, she can only climax if I make a screeching noise."

"Okay, yeah. That's unsettling."

"She doesn't even take her guns anymore. She only uses her sword. She says killing with her gun feels like sex with a condom. She likes to literally feel the life exit."

"I'm not sure what you want me to do, man. You know Kelley's backstory."

"Paul, listen, I want my Kelley back, I do. But there is a greater threat at play."

"What do you mean?"

"If Imperium can cause Kelley to revert to her old tactics

and her old way of thinking, they've won. They already have people all over the world descending into madness, embracing the darkness, or living in fear. At this rate, there won't be much of a world for UK and Pax to save."

"I know things look bleak. But what can we do but wait?"

"Kelley's answer to that question has been to sever the heads of as many torqs as possible. Every time she leaves, she comes home soaked in blood. I'm worried about her."

23

BING REN

U kweli did not sleep. The floor of the cave was too cold to sit on long enough to doze off and he couldn't find a suitable standing position that would relax his legs. So, he stood and stayed awake. All night. He moved his body periodically to keep warm and to make sure the beast knew he was still alive. The cave was too dark to see the beast clearly, Ukweli could only make out the reflection of sparse moonlight on the beast's bright white coat. Even in the darkness, he had no trouble locating the beast though. The baritone growl was present even in the jaguar's sleep. Ukweli hadn't dared to go any closer to the beast during the night for fear it might somehow accuse him of trying to get to his duffel. He couldn't afford any misunderstandings.

Ukweli was fully aware when the first light appeared at the entrance of the cave. The beast shook itself awake, fully rested after a long night of sleep, and stepped away from the backpack. *Great, I get to carry the supplies I'm not allowed to use.* Ukweli threw the pack in place and stepped into the light. He was immediately greeted by an icy wind that made him turn his shoulder, only to come face to face with the jaguar, a swift reminder there was no turning back.

Ukweli climbed. The jaguar followed closely. Ukweli climbed for hours, battling the wind and the frigid temperatures and the fatigue and the hunger. At one point, he swore he saw Hope but decided it was just a shadow. She had a way of showing up at his lowest moments, but she had not been present during the trials. He had needed to overcome the trials, without the presence of Hope.

As he climbed, Ukweli thought of Ava. He smiled when he thought of her killing the Black Swan's female attendants. He then thought it probably wasn't good he smiled when he thought of that. He thought of his mother and how she worked to try to give him and Uzuri a normal childhood under very abnormal circumstances. As he thought of his mother and his sister, a rage began to build in his spirit.

The Company had taken the most important people in his life. He had, in turn, embraced the darkness and submerged himself in the underworld inhabited by the Church of the Seer. It was that very same darkness that he was now experiencing on the edge of the mountain, and it made him stronger. He could see past the frigid gusts of wind. He now felt strength as he climbed. He could feel himself getting closer to Pax with every step. He was clear, focused, and angry. He no longer felt stalked by the jaguar. He had now assumed the mantle of leadership and the jaguar only served as his GPS. *Just show me the way, beast.*

Ukweli climbed. His lungs burned. His legs were heavy. His feet were numb. He just kept climbing. He fell. He took a breath. He stood. He climbed.

Suddenly, the jaguar let out a deafening roar and leaped over Ukweli and turned to face him. Ukweli drew his sword. "If this is how it ends, beast, so be it." The jaguar again roared loudly before approaching Ukweli. As Ukweli looked into the beast's blue eyes, they suddenly turned solid black. Ukweli's body went limp, and he fell to the ground with his sword still in his hand.

"Captain. Captain Aseyori." Ukweli could hear the voice, but he wasn't sure he could move. He opened his eyes but there was only darkness. The darkness was so dense, it was hard to tell that his eyes were open at all. He was warmer and he could smell smoke, so he knew a fire was near. He pushed down on his hands and sat up. He looked around but still, there was only darkness. "Welcome, captain." The voice seemed to come from all directions at once. It was clearly a man, but the voice wasn't deep. It was full of confidence and maturity. It was masculine yet nurturing. It was the voice of a man who had all he needed and feared nothing. Though they were in a cave, the voice had no echo. It was as clear as if the man were sitting right next to him.

"Bing Ren?"

"You've had quite a journey, friend. Fisk was very impressed with you. He thought for sure the swim would get you. His sword if not. Same with the Swan. Though, he was fairly upset with your lady friend. She's lively . . . full of passion, isn't she?"

"She is."

"Have you retrieved the artifacts?"

"I have." Ukweli reached into his pack and took out the small cup and the vial of water.

"Please, carefully pour the water into the cup and drink."

Ukweli followed the instructions. The vial began to glow as he poured what seemed only to be clear water into the metal cup. Ukweli raised the cup to his mouth, took a breath, closed his eyes, and drank the water. He found it to be refreshing. When he opened his eyes, he was sitting in a chair in green grass by a flowing river. "What . . . what is this place? Where am I?"

"This is the Dragon dimension. This is where your enemy has entrapped your loved ones and now prepares for your arrival. In order to rescue your family, you will need to travel here and defeat the Dragon."

Ukweli could not see Bing Ren. He could only hear his voice.

"How can I travel between dimensions? How do I get here?"

"Captain, it's time to go home. To travel to the Dragon dimension, you will need the device created by a team of Nobel laureates at Lagos University in Nigeria."

"My parents? The engine?"

"It's not an engine, but it is a device that enables travel . . . interdimensional travel, of course."

"My parents invented a time machine?"

"Technically your mother invented the device. And no, it's not a time machine. Time is of no consideration between dimensions. Time is a construct. It was created just like everything else. Rules govern every aspect of existence, so your mother learned that all created things can be manipulated by challenging those rules. She did, however, consider the device the worst mistake of her life as it came with dire consequences."

"Uzuri."

"To keep it out of the hands of dangerous people, and accessible by you alone, she locked the device away, protected by a riddle to confirm your identity. You will need to go to the university, solve the riddle, and acquire the device."

"Thank you, Bing Ren."

"Captain, be warned. Your enemy is formidable. It is only you that stands between the Dragon and the conquest he desires. You would be unwise to underestimate the power he draws from the fear and anger in the world."

"I won't."

The surroundings melted away and Ukweli once again found himself inside the cave. The jaguar was now standing face-to-face with Ukweli.

"Minnie can escort you down should you require it."

"No, thank you, I'll be—wait . . . you named this mammoth 'Minnie'?"

"What? She doesn't seem like a 'Minnie' to you?"

"No. Thank you though. And thank you, Minnie." The jaguar licked the side of Ukweli's face and turned and walked into the darkness of the cave.

(**24**)

THE CHURCH
RESPONDS

Ukweli sat in the chair at the head of the large conference table formerly occupied by Remington Cross. He felt the enormous weight of the position as he heard from his team concerning their battles with Imperium in his absence.

Ukweli looked around the table at the exhaustion in their faces. "How long have they had Paul and Kei?"

Alexander lifted his head. "It's been about two weeks now, I think."

"Do we know where they're holding them?" Ukweli tried unsuccessfully to hide the judgment in his voice.

"No. We're not even sure they're still in Atlanta."

"And what of Mendoza? Has anyone heard from her?"

"No. We haven't been able to contact her. Intel says they executed her in the city center, but we haven't been able to confirm it."

Kelley stood up. "You know, UK, things have been hard

for us here. I know you've been through a lot, with the trials and all, but Imperium unleashed hell on us, and we didn't have any miracles to save us. I don't even know how many torqs I've killed in the past few months. So, we've just been waiting for you to get the information you need to get to Pax so we can end this."

"I know, Kelley. I know. This has been hard on all of us, but we shouldn't start bickering now. We're as close as we've ever been to finding a real solution."

"So your mom hid this thing away, waiting for you to find it?"

"Yeah, she knew I would need it someday, but she knew Imperium wanted it too."

"So we have to go to Nigeria to get this device, right? Won't Imperium know we're trying to get it?"

"Imperium already knows." Ukweli spoke slowly and looked through Kelley. She glanced behind her to see what had his attention before returning her eyes to meet his.

"So you think they're just going to let us walk in there and get it?"

"Yes. We're going to walk in the front door and they're going to give us Paul and Kei."

OCTOBER 15, 2045

President James sat behind the desk in the oval office awaiting instructions from Jennifer. The president enjoyed his terms, largely devoid of major responsibilities or big decisions. He managed to amass a small fortune since becoming president, direct benefits of his submission to the leadership of Imperium, though he himself had never been inhabited. He generally just did what he was told and reaped the benefits of the position. He had been ordered to appear this morning cleanly shaven in a navy suit. He knew he would have a conversation with a terrorist, but he would only be repeating the words given to him in his earpiece. He needed to look tough. He needed to sound tough. He was pretty sure he could do it.

The oval office was full of people and cameras. There were lots of moving pieces. President James once thought to himself that he was glad he wasn't like one of those people. He had no desire to build a relationship with any of the White House civil servants. Plus, he was pretty sure he was a hero to them, and he sought never to allow them to become too familiar, thus sanding off a bit of the golden luster. In a way, he felt sorry for them. *Caught up in the rat race of life*, he thought to himself. He just showed up, did his job, and went home. *A model of efficiency*. He wasn't asked to be creative or thoughtful. No one expected empathy or even strength. It was all a performance, and he didn't mind.

The President's chief of staff walked over to him and put his left hand on his shoulder.

"Mr. President, do you have your script?"

"Yes. It's here somewhere."

The chief of staff laid a piece of paper on the desk in front of the President. "Here is another copy. Remember, just stick to the script. Captain Aseyori will try to manipulate your words. That's not a concern today, though, because you're just going to stick to the script, right?"

"Of course. Piece of cake. Stick to the script." He was looking at a portrait of Alexander Hamilton in the office and he began to think about how painful it must have been to die from a gunshot to the stomach.

At some point, when he wasn't paying attention, someone put an open laptop in front of him and said, "You have fifteen seconds, Mr. President. When the call comes in just click the red telephone on the screen."

President James awoke from his daydream and said, "What?" just as the large red phone icon appeared on the computer screen. "Oh, okay. Gotcha." He clicked the shimmering icon and a video feed appeared and the face of Ukweli Aseyori was on his screen.

"Good morning, Mr. President. You're looking sharp this morning, sir."

"Thank you, Captain Aseyori. I hope I'm dressed appropriately for such a special occasion."

"And what makes today so special, sir?"

"It's not every day that the world's most wanted terrorist arranges terms for surrender."

"Mr. President, please let the record show that the Church of the Seer is not responsible for the Sunday morning assassinations. We have only responded to the oppression instilled by the leaders of the Company and Imperium which, unfortunately, puts us at odds. I'm not your enemy, sir. I am certainly no enemy of the United States. I am, however, an enemy of Imperium."

"Then there is no need for further pleasantries. What terms do you propose?"

"I will turn myself in, along with Kelley, under the following conditions. I'll meet you or your representatives at the front door of the physics building at Lagos University in Nigeria. I'll agree to a prisoner swap. When I see my friends Paul and Kei walk out the doors and into safety, Kelley and I will walk in the doors, into your custody."

"What assurance do I have you'll show up once your friends have been freed?"

"How many thousands of agents have you lost trying to capture Kelley? I'm offering you a way to have us both in custody without the loss of resources. What do you have to lose?"

"Do you really think I'm going to let you get that close to the interdimensional engine?"

"The terms are as I have presented them. Take it or leave it. The choice is yours."

President James slowly closed the laptop and looked around the room. "So, how did I do?"

"Mr. President, how many times do we have to remind you to stick to the script?" The president's chief of staff put his hand on his forehead, took a hit from his vape, and started a slow clap. There were muffled sighs from different faces around the room, immediately followed by sporadic and uneasy applause.

25

LAGOS UNIVERSITY

OCTOBER 20, 2045

General Carter stood on the steps in front of the physics building at Lagos University. He was flanked by two hundred soldiers: one hundred outside on the lawn and one hundred inside the building. The general insisted that all two hundred soldiers be inhabited. He knew any non-torqs wouldn't survive to tell the tale anyway. There was a flash of light from the parking structure across the street.

"There's the signal. Bring 'em out."

The glass doors on the front of the building opened and Paul and Kei walked out. They were battered and worn but walked with pride and strength. They walked down the stairs and stood in front of the general. He raised his hand, revealing a magnetic device that released the large bracket cuffs. Paul rubbed the sore parts of his wrists. Kei's wrists were so worn the skin was broken and the blood ran into her hands, but she was much too prideful to rub them. She wouldn't dare give them the satisfaction of thinking they made her uncomfortable. The couple walked with a regal cadence to the parking structure across the street and disappeared. The general stood and waited for Ukweli and Kelley to appear, but there was no further movement. The general lifted his megaphone.

"Captain Aseyori!" He waited but there was no response. "Kelley Jack!" Again, no movement. Only silence. "Dammit, I knew it! I knew they would screw me over!" At that point, the frustrated general turned to face the building and was surprised to see Ukweli and Kelley standing in the doorway, holding the doors open.

"You coming inside, general?" Ukweli wore a sly smile the general wished he had the guts to slap off.

Ukweli and Kelley Jack sat opposite General Carter in the third-floor faculty lounge in the physics building at Lagos University. The silence was deliberate. Kelley and Ukweli awaited instructions from the general, but he was hesitant to speak, knowing the cunning possessed by the leaders of the Church. He insisted his silence would lead Kelley or Ukweli to give away valuable positioning. The longer they sat in silence, the more anxious the general grew. Eventually, he relieved himself and his lungs.

"Ok, Captain Aseyori, what's your angle?"

"Sir?"

"I know you had motive for turning yourself in."

"You took my friends captive for no reason."

"You lead a treasonous organization. We are well within our rights to apprehend any and all threats to the leadership of our nation."

"Our nation is being led by demons and corrupt humans. I will always stand against the threat of tyranny and oppression."

"Your motives are personal! You've blamed the Company for every bad thing that's ever happened to you and your family. You're blinded by rage, selfishness, and guilt."

"You're willingly inhabited by a demon that has twisted your thinking. You've seen rogue torqs, general. You've seen good men commit the most atrocious acts behind a debased mind."

"There is freedom in inhabitation, captain."

"What freedom exists in surrendering your mind?"

"It doesn't matter. The two of you won't be alive long enough for any of this to matter. Jennifer wanted me to wait until you cracked the code on the dimensional engine to kill you, but I'll have to explain to her that your soul was required." General Carter positioned himself right in front of Kelley. "I'll go down in history for being the single man who took down the Church of the Seer and the infamous Kelley Jack."

Kelley, in a single motion, stood and attacked the outside of the general's knee with a powerful downward kick. He screamed in pain and fell to the floor. As his back hit the tiled surface, the top piece of Kelley's high-heel boot made its way into the general's eye and through his head.

The one hundred fully inhabited soldiers began to pour into the room only to be quickly dispatched by the still magnetically cuffed members of the Church of the Seer. Ukweli and Kelley fought through the wave of incoming torqs with precision and aggression until Ukweli was able to remove the key from the general's breastplate to release himself and his fighting mate from the large cuffs as the glowing red lights on them turned pale blue.

As the pair continued to fight and win decisively, an inconspicuous ceiling tile in the corner of the room was removed and Ava dropped through the space onto the floor. She calmly walked to the nearest table and placed two swords and an assault rifle in an organized pattern.

"Hey, you guys need these or no?"

"Better late than never I guess, heh?" Ukweli spoke calmly as he twisted the head of an aggressive torq, snapping the assailant's neck and triggering the high-pitched squeal associated with the escaping demon as the used host fell to the floor. Kelley quickly grabbed her sword and gun and began to execute the soldiers two-by-two. Ukweli seized his sword and placed it in the sheath on his back, as he found taking lives by hand to be uniquely empowering. Ava slid a chair from under a nearby desk and sat, tapping her watch as she resisted the urge to remove her own pistol from its holster.

As the last of the torqs succumbed to the sword, barrel, and hands of the infamous prisoners, Ava walked to the closet labeled *Top Secret* and opened the doors. She pulled out a large suitcase and softly placed it on the table.

Ukweli winced. "Hey, be careful with that."

"It's not my first day, you know." Ava rolled her eyes, offended by the request. "So, how exactly does this work? There's a reason they haven't opened this thing in all this time."

Ukweli smiled. "They didn't open it because they couldn't open it."

"I'm surprised they left it here in Nigeria. They could've had their own scientists working on it in the US." Kelley untrustingly stayed away from the case as she spoke.

Ava continued to examine the case with a few different gadgets. "They couldn't take it out of this room. There's some sort of magnetic field around the case."

Kelley said, "So, what kept them from just ripping it open?"

Ukweli stood in front of the case. "Mara included a fail-safe." He opened the case and removed the metallic halo from the protective space in the lid. The remaining contents included a flat, steel layer with a keypad on the right side with numbers zero to nine and letters *a* to *z*, a digital display in the middle with spaces for ten figures, and a plaque on the left with the three lines of a haiku, which read:

You stood in the pool

Alas, not to go swimming

The river of life

"The haiku elicits a response between one and ten digits. A single incorrect entry begins a process whereby the engine destroys itself, so they couldn't afford to be wrong."

"Did you just say whereby? Damn, you're pretentious." This time it was Kelley's turn to roll her eyes.

Ava walked up behind Ukweli as he stood in front of his mother's invention. Ukweli began to think of the journey that led him to this place. He survived the trials and earned the right to return to Lagos and now he stood this close to a reunion with Pax. Ava placed her hand on his back.

"Babe, do you know the answer?"

"Yeah. I loved swimming growing up. You could always find Uzuri and me in or near a swimming pool for most of our childhood. But the last pool I stood in was definitely not for swimming." He engaged the small switch beside the keypad and the system powered on. A single tear rolled down his cheek as he typed the letters B-L-O-O-D.

There was the movement of small gears that released the metal plate. Ukweli grabbed the plate on both sides and carefully lifted it from its place. Underneath was a large cylinder with a single chrome switch on top.

Kelley looked around Ukweli's shoulder at the engine. "Could it be that simple? You just flip one switch?"

"I guess. One switch."

"What does the halo do?"

"It forms the neural connection that determines the destination. I saw the Dragon dimension during my meeting with Bing Ren. You guys will need to step outside."

Kelley started walking briskly. "You don't have to tell me twice."

Ava was more reluctant. "You don't know what's on the other side of this switch."

"Pax is on the other side of this switch. That's all I need to know." Ukweli carefully placed the halo on his head.

Ava said, "Good luck then," and walked out the door. Ukweli returned his attention to the machine and just before he flipped the switch, Ava stormed back into the room. She turned Ukweli toward her and kissed him deeply. She squeezed his body tightly and then let him go. She took a deep breath and said, "Please don't be mad, babe."

Ava pulled Ukweli's face toward her with her right hand on the back of his head and kissed him again. With her left hand, she flipped the switch. Kelley watched as there was a blinding flash of light and Ava and Ukweli disappeared.

(**26**)

THE SIMULATION

U kweli slowly opened his eyes, fighting the urge to close them quickly due to the extreme brightness of the environment. There were bright lights in the ceiling and the walls were painted a bright white. The floor was a shade of hot pink that provided a bizarre contrast and gave Ukweli the impression he was floating on the back of a flamingo. He was sitting in a chair positioned in front of a round table. There was a glass vase in the center of the table with a dozen white roses with white stems and white leaves.

Ukweli lifted his hands to see he wasn't bound in any way. He wore a pair of black jeans, black sandals, and a black T-shirt with red letters outlined in white that read *Mean People Suck . . . and I'm Mean*. Ukweli stood up to look around the room, but he didn't notice any windows or doors and sat back down once he started to feel lightheaded. He put his hands in his face and took a deep breath but looked up when he heard footsteps. His eyes were able to focus in time to see Jackson take a seat in the chair on the other side of the table.

"Congrats, UK. I honestly didn't think you could do it, yet here you are. Well, now that you're here, allow me to offer you a proper welcome."

There was immediate movement as men and women dressed in red brought out red plates, red cutlery, gold goblets with red trim, red candles with flames that burned green, and red silk napkins. The men poured a red liquid into the cups that made Ukweli think of the blood in the desert until Jackson took a sip and Ukweli decided Jackson would likely not drink blood, even as a dragon. Ukweli drank from his cup and was pleased to find that it was sweet and refreshing.

"It's dragon fruit juice. You see what I did there?"

Ukweli was moderately amused but did not smile. Jackson was dressed in all white and was wearing a shirt with red letters trimmed in black that read *Mean People Suck . . . and You're Mean.*

"You're really going to enjoy dinner. I got us a couple of tomahawks on the grill. Should be done in a few minutes. Until then, let me give you the rundown."

"Where is Pax?"

"He's safe. Don't worry. I must tell you, he's a very pleasant kid, Ukweli. You would've really loved raising him. He is so interesting."

Ukweli stood up and slammed his hands on the table, nearly knocking the candles over. "Listen, you take me to Pax right now or—"

"Or what, UK? What are you gonna do if I don't take you to Pax right now?"

Ukweli started to walk around the table toward Jackson when suddenly his body started moving in reverse. He walked backward, retracing his steps exactly, and sat down in the chair.

"What . . . what did you do to me?"

"UK, you're in the Dragon dimension. I created this place. I have complete control here. You can only do what I allow you to do. Which brings us to the first order of business. While I am impressed you survived everything you did to get here, it's not going to end the way you hoped. There won't be any heroic endings for you. You'll never see Pax again. You'll never see Kiera again—although she's been a pain in the ass. Maybe you two really are meant for each other."

"Jackson, where is—"

"Shhh. Don't interrupt, UK. I wasn't quite finished. Because you decided to bring your wife, Ava, on your escapade here, you'll have the unintended consequence of knowing she'll never see her loved ones again either. You brought that on yourself though, so, I don't really feel bad about that."

Two women dressed in red appeared and sat plates down in front of Ukweli and Jackson with large tomahawk steaks and asparagus spears.

"You know, UK, this is my favorite meal. I prepared this meal for myself the very night I planned on proposing to Kiera for the first time. I didn't get to do it, though, because you and your mates were playing in the Champions League final, and she was focused on the screen." Jackson took a bite. "In retrospect, there were quite a few red flags. I guess I was blinded by love. You have ruined my life in so many ways, but Kiera was the love of my life, and you took that from me. You destroyed any chance I had at ever being happy. And for what? You never loved her the way I did. She was crazy about you and all you ever did was ignore her and make her work to try to get close to you. I was so happy when she grew tired of your games and came to her senses, only to find you again after you followed us to Atlanta."

Ukweli wanted to speak but found he couldn't open his mouth.

"You seduced my wife, knocked her up, and threw her back out into the world, like a wounded gazelle, to fend for herself, hoping no one would be the wiser. But there's one thing you didn't see coming. You were far too arrogant to see it coming. The bottom line is, you're not as good as you think you are. You think you're fighting the good fight when you're actually just a bloodthirsty terrorist. You think you're a good person when you're actually full of darkness and hate. You think you're a good husband because no one else knows your secret; that you never stopped sleeping with my wife. I wonder how 'Loyal Ava' will react to that news. You've convinced yourself you're one of the good guys when you've inflicted far more pain on the world than the world has on you."

Jackson made a circular hand motion freeing up Ukweli's ability to speak.

"Jackson, you know I've loved Kiera for a long time. I never meant to hurt you or Ava, or Kiera. Okay, so you've been hurt. That doesn't excuse you from taking the life force from innocent people to support your own selfish ambitions."

"Captain Aseyori!" Jackson struggled to speak for laughing. "My selfish ambitions! Do you hear yourself? Did you not, just seconds before you hit the switch on the engine, reject the use of your katana so you could continue killing with your bare hands? Accept it, UK. You're the antagonist in this story. I'll be a hero once I dispose of you, and I'll finally be able to take my rightful place as the benevolent ruler of a grateful planet."

"If you hate me so much, why all of this? Why not just kill me?"

"Oh, trust me, I will kill you in due time."

"But not now, huh? Is it because you aren't the ultimate authority, even in a dimension that you created for yourself?"

"While the Magician does possess a small measure of influence, he can't help you here. I will kill you when I get good and ready."

"Okay, Jackson, how does this work? When do we do this?"

"Ahh, UK. You will have to learn to be careful with your words. Don't be in a rush, though. You haven't even touched your food. Don't be rude. Eat up."

"I'm not hungry."

"I insist."

Ukweli, involuntarily, began to cut his steak and eat.

"While you eat, I'll explain. You have entered what I call the Simulation. You and I will fight every day in the stadium in front of my loyal subjects. If you're able to beat me or kill me, you win. I'll release you, Pax, Kiera, and Ava and you can all return to your own dimension to live as you please. I feel like I should warn you though. The world is in complete disarray. The Beautiful One is running rampant through the minds of the citizens and chaos is the order. By the time you get back, all your friends will be dead. The world will no longer exist as you remember it." Jackson picked up a single asparagus spear and ate it in fifteen small bites.

"And if I don't kill you?"

"Well, if I win, you, Kiera, Pax, and Ava will remain here with me forever. Losing forever. You'll never see them. You'll just lose every day and return here where you will be served hand and foot . . . alone. Everyday."

"So your plan is to beat me, every day, without killing me?"

"Yes. As it turns out, that is quite the dilemma for me. You see, the Simulation only ends with a blood sacrifice. The Simulation will come to an end the day I kill you."

"What if I kill myself? Would the others be released from your Simulation?"

"Geez, you're so dramatic. I can't imagine what she sees in you. No, UK, you can't kill yourself. If you die by any means, other than my hands, your wife, your child, and your strumpet will remain here in my service forever."

"So if we fight every day, but you can't kill me, how do we know who wins the day?"

"Oh, that's the best part. Our duals will consist of one three-minute round daily. If you're not able to overtake me in the three minutes, the judges will decide who wins."

"The judges?"

"Yes. My loyal subject will rotate onto the panel of judges and they will decide who has won."

"So, basically, every day I don't kill you, you win."

"Basically, yes."

"When do the bouts begin?"

"Now." A large group of men and women quickly removed the plates, cups, cutlery, candles, flowers, and the table and chairs. Only the chair Ukweli sat in remained. Jackson stood, took off his shirt, and held out his arms while a man covered his hands in athletic tape. Ukweli tried to stand but found himself unable to move. He sat in the chair with his arms by his side. The walls fell down to reveal a large arena with ten thousand "fans" already seated. There was the sound of a bell and Jackson began to punch Ukweli in the face, arms, chest, and stomach while the rabid crowd cheered wildly. For three minutes, Ukweli sat, unable to fight back, while Jackson delivered blow after blow to Ukweli's body. When the bell rang, Ukweli sat bloody and bruised in the chair, still unable to move. It was only after a voice over the public address system announced Jackson as the winner that Ukweli's body went limp and he fell out of the chair and onto the floor. Suddenly, the walls returned to their place and Ukweli was in the room, on the floor, bloody, and alone.

Ukweli slowly opened his eyes as the glare from the bright incoming sunlight was seemingly ordered to offend his corneas. He blinked as he sat up on the side of the bed and looked around. There was a very familiar feel to his surroundings and Ukweli couldn't decide if it was déjà vu. Suddenly, it came to him, and he realized he was sitting on the edge of the bed in his downtown Green Wood apartment in Tottenham. He hadn't been there since his permanent move to Atlanta to join the Church. He stood up and walked to the balcony and watched the people moving briskly toward the park. He walked back inside and went into the bathroom and looked in the mirror. There was no blood on his face. No marks or bruises. *How is this possible? Where am I?* Just then the phone rang. He walked into the kitchen and lifted the receiver.

"Hello?"

"Good morning, captain. Did you rest well?"

"Who is this?"

"Apologies. I am Camille Blanchet. I'm your personal concierge. I am here to help you as you learn to navigate the Simulation."

"How did I get here, to London?"

"It was the opinion of DayStar that you would likely feel most comfortable in your Tottenham loft. Any discomfort in your experience can affect your acceptance of the Simulation."

"Wait, am I actually in London?"

"No, sir."

"What happened to the bruises on my face?"

"The physical damage to your person will always reset when the Simulation resets the day."

"Resets the day?"

"Yes, sir. At the end of your contests with DayStar, the Simulation will reset your day. This will always include a restoration of your physical person."

"But I remember everything that happened. I vividly remember the first contest."

"Yes, sir. DayStar decided you would provide a greater degree of challenge and thus a greater level of entertainment if you were allowed to compile your experiences."

"So, if I'm not in Tottenham, where am I?"

"You're in the same room as before." The surroundings began to pixelate and eventually melted down to reveal white walls. It was the same room he woke up in after Ava flipped the switch on the machine in Lagos. "You see? DayStar just wants to make you as comfortable as possible, since you're going to be with us for a while."

"A while?"

"Yes, sir. Well, technically, *a while* would suggest the passing of time here, which is also only a part of the Simulation. The time construct you experience in your world is not applicable here, but DayStar is interested in giving you the most authentic exposure. So, you will feel as though days are passing even though there is no actual progression of time."

"But time continues to pass normally on Earth?"

"Yes, sir."

"And the only way I can end the simulation is to kill Jackson, correct?"

"Yes, sir. You will need to defeat DayStar in a competition. Point of emphasis. It is not possible for you to defeat DayStar. The judges will rule in his favor even if it seems you have decisively won, and he reserves the right to reset the day at any point. The Simulation only ends with a blood sacrifice, so unless he kills you, which he won't do, or you defeat him, which you can't do, it will continue forever. That is why DayStar wants you to be comfortable. You will be with us for *a while*."

"And what happens to Earth?"

"I am only allowed in the briefings concerning this dimension, but the Company still controls the activity in your world. They have quite the footing there and things seem to be going as planned. Of course, madness, darkness, and chaos probably doesn't sound like a good plan to you but it's right in line with the mission of the Beautiful One."

"Where is my family? Where is Pax?"

"Your family is also experiencing the Simulation. They are safe and comfortable."

"When is my next fight?"

"Now."

The walls melted away and Ukweli was once again in the ring in the stadium. This time, however, he wasn't cuffed. His hands were taped, and he was free to move. Jackson stood at the opposite corner and shouted obscenities. There was a bell and Jackson moved aggressively toward Ukweli, who dodged his first punch and returned with a powerful counter followed quickly by a leg sweep and a heel to the midsection as he lay crouching. Jackson slowly rose to his feet and charged again, only to be met with a front kick, followed by a roundhouse to the side of the face.

Ukweli moved in closely and began to issue body shots to the chest and abdomen before dropping to punch the inside of Jackson's left knee. Jackson buckled and retreated but Ukweli followed with a flying scissor punch to Jackson's temple. Jackson fell to the canvas.

Medical personnel entered the ring to tend to Jackson along with three large men who backed Ukweli into the corner opposite where Jackson lay. There was a bell and the public announcer spoke. And the winner by unanimous decision . . . DayStar! The referee lifted Jackson's hand but, because he was unconscious, his arm flopped back down by his side.

"What?!" Ukweli was furious, but the men held him firmly. Suddenly, he was in his bed in his apartment in the Green Wood neighborhood of Tottenham. The sun was rising. It was a new day. The phone rang.

"Camille?"

"Good morning, captain. Did you rest well?"

"Camille, Jackson was unconscious on the floor of the ring, yet he still won."

"Yes, sir. I'm afraid the judges weren't very fair to you. You fought very well. Outstanding speed and intimidating ferocity."

"So, what happens now?"

"Perhaps you would like breakfast. I would suggest the buffet. They have crab claws and there is an omelet station."

"When does my next fight begin?"

"Now." Ukweli was in the ring in the stadium. His hands were taped. The bell rang and Jackson charged aggressively. Ukweli tackled him to the ground and rolled him into a leg lock. Ukweli pushed down on Jackson's upper ankle until he heard the knee joint pop. Jackson screamed in pain as Ukweli rolled him into a reverse broomstick. The bell rang and the crowd cheered as the referee lifted Jackson's hand as he writhed in pain on the floor of the ring.

The sun pierced the blinds. The phone rang.

"Good morning, Camille."

"Good morning, captain. Did you rest well?"

"When is my next fight?"

"Now." Ukweli was in the ring in the stadium.

The sun pierced the blinds. The phone rang.

"Good morning, Camille."

"Good morning, captain. Did you rest well?"

"I did Camille, thank you."

"Perhaps you would like breakfast?"

"You know, Camille, I've been meaning to try the buffet. I heard they have crab claws and an omelet station."

"Excellent choice, sir." Ukweli hung up the phone and walked out of the apartment to the elevator. The music in the elevator was soul from the 1960s. Ukweli sang along. Ukweli stepped out of the elevator feeling upbeat and optimistic. He walked through the lobby and greeted the attendant just before walking outside. Ukweli looked around at the Tottenham community going about their day and strolled across the street to a building with a large neon sign that read *Breakfast Buffet*. Ukweli walked inside to find a sports bar with his career highlights on the screens. He was greeted by fans as he walked through the restaurant before he was grabbed by a member of the wait staff who guided him to the VIP area. Ukweli took a seat.

"We've prepared crab claws and an omelet for you. Please let us know what else you might like from the buffet, and we'll bring it right to you." The waiter placed two plates in front of Ukweli, one with six large stone crab claws and the other with a four-egg wagyu filet omelet with grilled onions and truffle gravy.

"Maybe I can try the cheese grits and I'll have a bit of the corned beef hash."

"Perfect. And what would you like to drink, sir?"

"Please bring me a glass of water and your finest apple juice."

"Excellent. Would you like bread?"

"What do you have?"

"Everything, sir. We have biscuits, toast, bagels, cornbread, muffins, rolls, and anything else you might like. Just let us know."

"Awesome. Thank you."

Ukweli dove in, and still had the crab cracker in his hand, his lips glistening from the clarified butter, when a beautiful young woman walked over to his table and stood in front of him. She was tall and slender with light brown skin and black hair. Her hazel eyes seemed to stare through him. He was captivated. She almost reminded him of . . .

"What do you think of our breakfast buffet so far, captain?" Ukweli recognized the voice.

"Camille?"

"Yes, sir."

"Ah, it's very nice to meet you — well, in person I mean."

"Yes, sir."

"Have you had breakfast, Camille? Would you like to join me for crab claws and omelets?"

"Thank you, sir, but I'm afraid not. We really aren't allowed to participate in your experience aside from making sure you have everything you need."

"Nonsense. You just said it's my experience, right? If so, then I insist you join me for breakfast." Ukweli lifted his hand and snapped his finger twice. "Garçon, a place for the young lady, please."

"Of course, sir. My pleasure."

Camille sat down across from Ukweli, and the waiter brought her a napkin, a glass of water, and a bowl of mixed fruit. Ukweli stuffed his face with egg and crab and corned beef hash and narrated his highlights for Camille. She seemed genuinely interested. Once Ukweli was full, the staff cleared the table and returned with a cart of delectables. There were cinnamon rolls, French toast, pancakes, and a number of other ooey-gooey treats for Ukweli to try. Feeling almost childlike, Ukweli rubbed his hands together and imagined himself saying, *I don't mind if I do.* He just hummed instead.

"Sir, might I recommend the waffles?" Ukweli stopped eating and dropped his utensils. He looked at Camille to gauge her intentions. Her expression didn't change. He was quickly reminded of his situation and warned himself not to let his guard down.

"I think I'll try the cinnamon roll, please."

"Excellent, sir."

Ukweli ate the cinnamon roll. It was covered in a sweet, creamy sauce. It was delicious. He leaned back in his seat and looked over at Camille.

"You really should've tried the cinnamon roll."

"Yes, sir. I've had them before. They are quite tasty."

"So, Camille, what's your story?"

"I'm not sure I understand, sir."

"I mean, what's your story? How did you end up here?"

"You mean, here, in this dimension, sir?"

"Yes."

"I was born here."

"You were born in the Dragon dimension?"

"Yes, sir. We all were. DayStar is the creator of all things. He is our father, and it is our honor to serve him."

"So, your service to me is an extension of your service to DayStar?"

"Yes, sir."

Ukweli chuckled. *Yeah, I've heard that before,* Ukweli thought to himself. He picked up his napkin and cleaned his mouth and hands. "Camille, this has been a lovely breakfast. Thank you for the recommendation and for the honor of your company."

"Of course. It was my pleasure, sir."

"Camille."

"Sir?"

"When is my next fight?"

"Now."

"Hello, Camille. Good morning."

"Good morning, captain. Did you rest well?"

"I guess, but I'm really not sure. If time is truly a construct that doesn't exist here, then there hasn't been a night and I didn't actually sleep. Though I feel rested, it's only because my mind is convinced I have experienced a nocturnal cycle. So, I guess, to answer your question, my simulated rest was satisfying."

"And would you like breakfast?"

"Thank you, Camille, but I'm fine this morning. Let's just get to it."

"Sir?"

"When is my next fight, Camille?"

"Now."

The walls dissolved and Ukweli was in the ring in the stadium with Jackson standing in the opposite corner. Ukweli walked over to Jackson who seemed concerned and annoyed by Ukweli's deviation from the routine.

"Jackson—uhh, DayStar, why do we always fight in the same place? Can we consider a change of scenery?"

"What exactly did you have in mind, UK?" Ukweli smiled as the scene changed to the dojo at Highgate School.

"I remember being frustrated because I didn't know what my headaches were about. Then I found out you were possessed by a demon. It really boosted my confidence to know you knew you couldn't beat me on your own."

"UK, brother, have you forgotten I'm undefeated against you in this dojo?"

"Jackson, have you forgotten I've done nothing but dominate you since Thysia leveled the playing field?"

Jackson's eyebrows hinged and his face turned red. "Ring the bell."

As usual, Jackson led aggressively and approached Ukweli with an opening barrage of punches. He was very strong and his punches, even the ones that didn't land cleanly, took a toll. Jackson moved up and down with his head and landed kicks to Ukweli's lower leg. Ukweli countered with upper body shots and a swinging gate punch to Jackson's inner thigh that made a bruise. Jackson moved in to grapple and the two locked arms. Ukweli spun quickly and threw Jackson to the ground where the two of them fought for positioning. Jackson fought to turn and eventually got Ukweli on his back and delivered an elbow blow to Ukweli's chin. He dropped a sharp elbow shot to Ukweli's chest that made him cough blood. Jackson quickly stood and delivered five quick kicks to Ukweli's ribcage that made him roll over into a fetal position.

"You chose this place, UK. You chose to return to the place where I learned to own my opponents, including you. This beating is all on you." Jackson kicked him again and again. He knelt over him and punched him in the jaw and the face until both his jaw and his nose were broken. "It's time for you to feel all of the pain you've caused me." Jackson punched Ukweli in his lower back repeatedly as Ukweli screamed in pain.

"I have no sympathy for you, UK." Jackson sat on the floor of the dojo and pulled Ukweli up just in front of him. He wrapped his arm around Ukweli's neck and began to squeeze. It gave Jackson great pleasure to see Ukweli squirm to fight for air.

"See, UK. The cream always rises to the top. Oh, and don't worry. As you feel yourself losing consciousness, I promise I will reset your day before you die. I'm sure you thought you could arouse my emotions by fighting here but, as always, I'm ten steps ahead of you, old friend. We'll get a chance to do this all over again."

Jackson squeezed with all his might, hoping he might break Ukweli's larynx. He only released the pressure when something got his attention. It was a sound, but it wasn't natural. It was as if a bullfrog was singing to the buzz of a hummingbird's wing beats. It was subtle but deafening. Jackson released Ukweli and stood up and started backing away.

"What is this? What is happening?" There was no response. Only the sound. "Reset the day. Reset the day now!" No movement. Only the sound. The day did not reset. Jackson rushed to Ukweli, who lay unconscious on the floor, to check his pulse. He was alive, barely. "Reset the day! He's still alive! Reset the day!"

Camille walked into the room from a dark corner. "The Simulation is over. The sacrifice has been accepted."

"That's impossible, Camille! I didn't kill him! He's still alive! No, no, the Simulation is not over. Reset the day!"

"Sir, I'm sorry. The Simulation is over. The sacrifice has been accepted."

"Sacrifice? What sacrifice?!"

The scene melted away and developed into a serene, grassy lift adjacent to a calm river of clear water. There were flowers of different colors and a beautiful sunset. Ukweli regained consciousness and managed to sit up against a tree. He could see out of one eye, but he could not speak. Jackson looked around, confused and frustrated.

"Why are we here, Camille? What's going on?"

"Sir, this is the Simulation of Ava, the captain's wife."

"So?"

"In order for her to accept the Simulation, we gave her access to see the captain in your contests. It gave her great pleasure to see him fight. She was greatly disturbed, though, by the parameters you set for the exit strategy."

"The exit strategy?"

"Yes, sir. She knew that no matter what he did, regardless of how well he fought, he couldn't win. So, she took it upon herself to win for him."

"What do you mean, win for him?"

Camille pointed to a small patch of mixed-colored roses. Lying there, in the midst of the ambrosial bouquet, was Ava, the captain's wife, lifeless in a small concrete basin slowly filling with blood, her delicate hands still gripping the African blackwood handle of the dagger plunged deep into her abdomen.

Jackson let out a primal scream as he stomped over to the tree where Ukweli was sitting up, aware of the dramatic turn of events. Ukweli struggled to breathe as one of his broken ribs punctured his lungs. He was in far too much pain to cry, not that it mattered since his body was incapable of making tears.

"You did this to me! You did this to me again!" Jackson lifted his right leg and aimed his heel toward Ukweli's forehead.

Ukweli startled himself awake in his apartment in Atlanta and looked around to see if a phone would ring. He had been lying on the couch when he sat up and checked his body for damage. There was no pain. He lifted his chin and looked around. He stood up and ran toward the bedroom.

"Ava! Ava!" Ukweli looked frantically for his wife. He checked the bathroom. He called for her. She wasn't there. He ran back into the living room and was surprised to see Hope.

"Oh no."

"Hello, Ukweli. Welcome back."

"Hope . . . no, no, no . . ."

"Ukweli, please, try to breathe."

"Just tell me. Is she gone?"

"Ukweli . . ."

"Hope! Is Ava gone?"

"Yes."

Ukweli grabbed a ceramic mug from the kitchen island and threw it at the sliding patio door. The collision shattered the mug and the door, and the glass fell to the floor as Ukweli fell to his knees. He began to sob loudly as he muttered his wife's name. "*Ava . . . Ava.*"

Hope sat down on the floor beside Ukweli and placed her hand on his back.

"Hope, why? Why did she do this?"

"She did what she did to save you."

"I didn't need saving!"

"She thought you did."

"She was wrong!"

"Ukweli, Ava did what she did because she loves you. She did what she did because she believes in you."

"What am I supposed to do now? I can't do this without her!"

"Ukweli, the world needs you now more than ever."

"I need Ava!"

"Ava served her purpose. She got you through the trials and out of the Dragon dimension. Her work is done. Yours isn't."

"I'll never see her again."

"She'll meet you in Caelum. Ava is in perfect peace resting in the shadow of the light of Thysia. You will see her again."

"Hope, I just . . ." Ukweli lifted his head. Hope was gone. Ukweli was startled by a knock at the door. He stood up and walked to the front door. "Kiera . . ."

"Shhhh, don't talk right now." She kissed Pax on the cheek and handed him to Ukweli. He took Pax and held him close to his chest and cried.

27

THE DUEL AT CITY CENTER

DECEMBER 31, 2045

The full unit gathered at the office and each team member was surprised to find there was no resistance. No one met torqs. No one had to fight their way out into the streets or into the building. The team was seated around the table when Ukweli walked into the room. He was holding Pax and Kiera walked behind him. Kelley jumped up from her chair.

"Well, how do you like this? You just couldn't wait to get your grimy hands on UK, could you? She was probably working with Jackson the whole time! She probably killed Ava herself! I should cut your throat right here and now!"

Ukweli responded, "Settle down, Kelley. Kiera's been through a lot too. We all have."

"Really. UK? What has she been through? What has she lost? She has Pax and, now that Ava is out of the picture, she has you. She couldn't have written a better storybook ending."

Kiera sighed and began to massage her temples. "Kelley, I don't care if you don't trust me. I don't care if you don't like me. But you knew Ava well enough to know she was her own woman. Do you really think I, or anyone, could've made her do something she didn't want to do?"

Kelley slowly returned to her seat.

Ukweli spoke calmly, attempting to relieve the tension. "Kelley, please. Let's not turn on each other. We need to figure out what's going on with Imperium. Why was there no opposition this morning? What are they planning and what does it have to do with Pax? Has there been any further word concerning Mendoza?"

Charlotte answered, "No. Nothing. We haven't confirmed it, but she's certainly dead by now."

The laptop on the desk began to buzz. Charlotte checked the screen. "You have an incoming call. It's from Jackson."

"Put it on the big screen." The two center plates on the front wall split in two and the red phone icon shimmied back and forth on the large display. Ukweli touched the icon. Jackson appeared on the screen.

"Jackson."

"Good morning, UK. Good morning, Seers."

"Where is Mendoza?"

"UK, I know it's none of my business, but why do you think you have to have all the girls, bruh? I really hate to say this, mainly because you're such a terrible person and I loathe you in so many ways for so many reasons, but you definitely have game, sir. The fact that you managed to come back from Mongolia with your wife AND your new girlfriend is astonishing. All while simultaneously convincing MY wife that she's important to you. You're a bad boy, UK."

"Jackson. Where is she?"

"She's fine, probably. She's . . . I don't know, somewhere around here. I mean, we don't have a dungeon, per se, but if we did, that's likely where she would be."

"Well, how about this. Why don't you tell me where you are, and I'll come see you."

"How exciting! That sounds cool, but I have a better idea. It's actually the reason I called."

"We're listening."

"I can admit I was furious when Ava ended the Simulation. I had you right where I wanted you and she bailed you out. You know, she really saved your skin a few times, didn't she?"

"Jackson."

"Okay, listen. Meet me outside the stadium tonight at eleven p.m. You and your team. We'll have a real duel, and I can bring in the new year with your head on a stick. After all, the best way to begin a new dynasty is with a big opening win."

"The last time you invited me to a duel I ended up in the Dragon dimension."

"Yeah, I had Pax then though. I don't think you're quite into Mendoza enough to chase her back into the Simulation. Unless, of course, you are. In which case, we can skip the chit-chat and get right to it."

"So, just you and me? One on one?"

"One on one. Be assured, though. I'll kill you while your team watches. Then we'll kill your team. Then I'll be happy to kill Kiera. I may keep Mendoza for myself. Boy, she'll do, am I right? Seriously though, are you really sleeping with her too? Where do you find the energy? Ginseng? Do you have some concoction from a Nigerian witch doctor?"

"Jackson, focus please."

"See? That's the best part." Jackson's eyes became red like

fire and the Dragon silhouette materialized behind him. "I'm always focused." The feed ended.

Paul spoke up. "You know it's a trap. Mendoza's likely dead already."

"I agree," Charlotte spoke from behind the desk. "It's a suicide mission."

Ukweli shook his head. "There's no need in prolonging the inevitable. It has to be done."

Kelley said, "Even if you beat him there's no guarantee they'll release her. I'm all for taking the Dragon's head, but at what cost? There has to be another way."

"You're right, all of you. It's definitely a trap. But there is no other way." Ukweli sat in his chair at the head of the table. "Plus, unfortunately, Mendoza isn't the only one who is counting on us tonight."

"What do you mean?"

Ukweli looked at Charlotte at the back of the room. "Hey, replay that conversation please."

Charlotte punched a key sequence, and the video conference began to replay.

"Look, there. Behind Jackson. The screen on the wall."

Kelley peered. "It's the itinerary for the New Year's Eve festivities tonight."

"They have a very special guest making a cameo."

Kelley looked closer and gasped as she read. "The Beautiful One will honor us with his presence at midnight. They're going to sacrifice the missing children?"

Alexander said, "So in addition to Mendoza, there are one hundred children whose lives are on the line as well."

"Seers, this has officially become a full-team rescue mission. Do whatever you have to do to get ready. I'm gonna beat Jackson's ass. You guys have to get those kids out of there."

As the team dispersed to prepare, Kiera approached Ukweli and handed Pax to him. She sat in the chair beside him and placed her elbow on the table and her chin in her hand.

"How are you feeling?"

"I feel fine but, honestly, I wish Ava were here. She always gave me confidence in crazy situations like this."

"I'm sorry that I can't be that for you."

"Don't apologize. Ava was one of a kind."

Kiera watched Ukweli as he looked at Pax and she wondered if he still loved her outside of the fact that she bore his child. She knew that she could never live up to the standard Ava set, and now she wondered if there was a place in Ukweli's life for her at all.

The more she watched Ukweli, the more she loved him.

The more she loved him, the more vulnerable she felt.

The more vulnerable she felt, the more insecure she became.

"So, you and Mendoza, huh?"

"Kiera, are you serious?"

"She is well built . . . very pretty . . . exotic features."

"So?"

"And smart. You guys have a lot in common."

"Kiera . . ."

"And she completely dropped her life in Mongolia to follow you to Atlanta."

"She didn't follow me to Atlanta. She followed Ava to Atlanta."

Kiera put her hand up to her mouth and gasped. "Did Ava know about the two of you?"

"There's nothing to know. I've never slept . . . why am I having to explain this to you right now?"

"I apologize for my insecurities, UK, but knowing what I

know about you and Ava, and listening to Jackson talk about you and Mendoza . . . I can't help but notice that you're willing to risk it all for her."

"Kiera, I came to the Dragon dimension for you."

"Ukweli, you came to the Dragon dimension for Pax."

"There is no Pax without you."

"Just tell me, UK."

"Tell you what?"

"What's going on between you and Mendoza?"

"Absolutely nothing."

"Then why are you putting your life in jeopardy to save her?"

"I'm the reason she's in trouble in the first place. She trusts me and she needs me."

"Pax needs you. I need you."

"Do you want me to just let her die?"

"Better her than you."

"This isn't just about Mendoza. You know I have to face Jackson sooner or later. The longer I wait, the more powerful he becomes. Fear is dominating our world and he feeds off it. If I can't defeat him now, it may already be too late."

"Look, UK, I want to be there for you, but I don't know who you are right now. I don't know what you need so I don't know how to help. I feel like I can't trust you and I'm certainly not Ava. I'm never going to just figure it out. So please, just tell me what to do."

"Just take care of Pax. For now, that's enough."

The convivial atmosphere at City Center was representative of any modern metropolitan area as the clock approached the twenty-third hour and the promise and un-certainty of a new year stood lurking right around the cor-ner. Thousands gathered on the streets and enjoyed live music and exotic food choices. Plenty of room was made for vices to flourish. The patrons pounded premium cocktails and imported lager while being amazed by the skill and precision of the engineers of the mega-drones that provided a large, bright countdown clock high in the night sky that would eventually morph into a giant peach during the final minute of the year.

The missing children were untouchables. Most of them were taken from orphanages or traded for drugs or other basic goods at the flourishing human trafficking posts in the Underground. Many of them were abandoned in those very alleys so they learned to survive in the Underground on their own, but they became easy targets for the Company's December Holiday Season manipulations. Some of them were just taken off the street, lured with candy or food or clothes or lies. The older children were tasked with helping to care for their younger counterparts, and they were so un-aware, or desperate, that they very often helped to recruit friends or others into the tragedy. This was their big night. This was their ultimate moment. When the giant drone peach would finally make its way down to touch the top of the dome stadium, the crowd would cheer and share kisses with loved ones or perfect strangers, the fireworks would explode, and the children would be poured into the massive fire pit, a burnt offering to celebrate the presence of the Beautiful One.

Once the planning and preparation were done, the team spent their evening in different ways. Paul and Kei went to the lounge adjacent to the weapons depot and enjoyed each other. Adam went to the gym to work off excess energy. He didn't mind fighting torqs or taking on Imperium, but there was something about Jackson and the Dragon form that gave him pause. He wasn't afraid of Jackson, but any hesitation could cost the whole team, so he knew he couldn't afford to be nervous. Charlotte stayed logged into the systems and monitored the comms for movement while doing her best to keep Pax entertained. Kelley and Alexander went to the outdoor platform on the fifteenth floor and watched the sunset. She lay her head in his lap and he brushed and braided her hair while she cleaned her guns and sharpened her sword. He sang while he twisted the strands of her hair.

Ukweli split his time between the dojo and the chapel. Kiera watched closely, captivated by his movements, as he did tai chi. She loved watching him work since they were in high school together in Islington. She felt the urge to speak, but she didn't want to interrupt the moment.

When he finished his training, his countenance invited her to join him in the shower. The two of them enjoyed each other as much as they ever had. They dressed and transitioned to the chapel where Kiera sat behind Ukweli and applied organic vanilla and cocoa oils to his body as he meditated on a mat on the floor. Kiera paid detailed attention to the various scars that covered his legs and abdomen as she realized the toll the trials took on him. *Ava was here for all of this. This is why he loved her so much.* She dreaded having to let him go into the city. She wanted to sit on the floor and touch him forever.

The strike team from the Church of the Seer, the single most elite unit in the world, was prepared to go to battle with its most formidable opposition yet. They knew how to fight and shoot, but they all realized the unique challenge of facing an opponent with supernatural abilities. They came together and Alexander covered them in prayer before they loaded the transports and headed toward the city center. Ukweli traveled alone on his cycle. He generally enjoyed battling torqs with his ancient uchigatana, but he traveled with two modern katanas attached to his armor in the back. He simply couldn't afford to take chances tonight.

As he sped toward the stadium, he remembered his contests with Jackson at Highgate and in the Dragon dimension. He replayed Jackson's fighting style in his mind, and he wondered if his preparation would matter, given Jackson's newfound abilities. As he got closer to the stadium, he noticed the increase in foot traffic, and by the time he was a kilometer away, the reaction from the bystanders let him know Imperium knew he was there. He went to the comms.

"Squad, it looks like it's go-time. They're not just gonna let me drive up to the front door, so I'll have to fight my way in. Watch out for each other and get those kids out of there. UK out."

Ukweli sped through the crowds until he began taking on gunfire. He drew his sword and began to carve his way toward the area with the bright lights where he knew Jackson would be waiting for him. The closer he got, the greater the number of torqs, and the fighting was heavy. He suddenly noticed someone riding a bike beside him, fighting alongside him. He looked over and was slightly startled when she spoke into his comms.

"They have plasma cannons around the corner! Get ready to jump!"

"What?! Unity?!"

"Jump! Now!"

Ukweli replaced his sword, braced himself, pressed down hard on the foot pedals, and launched himself into a backward somersault. Unity lifted her feet and pressed down on the back of her seat, propelling her body upward with her elbows high and her knees pressed against her chest. The cannons fired, directly striking and destroying the bikes under them. Unity landed, rolled, and began to attack and dismantle the cannons. Ukweli landed, drew both swords, and began to strike down torqs as they approached in waves. The hissing sound was music to his ears and he was aware he was smiling as he fought. This was nothing like the trials. This was why he was born. He was finally home. Ukweli slashed his way through two units of torqs before coming face-to-face with Jackson.

DayStar wore a red suit and gold-trimmed sunglasses.

"Are you good and warmed up, UK? No excuses this time."

"We're not in the Dragon dimension anymore, Jackson. Your reign ends now."

Kelley and the strike team managed to enter the bowels of the stadium undetected only to have Hope purposely trigger an alarm, raising the unit's awareness of the imminent threat, summoning four units of torqs. The Seers used their guns, all except for Kelley, who exclusively slayed with her sword. Adam and Paul led the way as they kicked and punched in between gunshots while Charlotte and Kei worked the perimeters and took down strays and eliminated the possibility of opponents flanking. When the movement stopped, Hope reappeared.

"This way. Hurry." The team followed Hope around two corners and down three flights of stairs, into an opening where the abducted children were being held in cages.

"We're gonna get you out of here." Kelley went to the first

cage, shot the lock, and removed the chains before opening the cage door. Her rage caused her to flashback to a time in her childhood when she was punished for a classroom mistake with an afternoon in the basement cage and she vowed to seek the freedom of enslaved children all over the world. Just like she rewarded her molester with ninety-nine stab wounds as a young girl, she sought to honor those who perpetuated child slavery with a taste of the cold edge of her steel.

As the team broke the cage doors and escorted the children to safety, Kei noticed a large cage in the corner and discovered Mendoza, exhausted and severely dehydrated, lying on the cold dirty floor. She broke open the cage and tried to arouse Mendoza with water and salt, but she lay still. Kei softly whispered in her ear, "Ukweli needs you." Mendoza coughed and rolled over.

Hope said, "We need to get the children to the Underground. They must find as many of their friends and family as they can and bring them back here. Ukweli needs our help."

Jackson drew his sword. Ukweli sheathed the sword in his left hand and walked toward Jackson. His walk became a jog, and his jog became a sprint. Ukweli quickly closed the space between them and their swords clashed and the searing sound of razor edges cross-connecting shattered the glass of a nearby vehicle. Ukweli dropped to his knees and his momentum carried him beyond Jackson on his first pass. He immediately rose to his feet and reengaged. Jackson seemed unbothered and made strong, deliberate motions with his sword. Feigning boredom, Jackson responded to

Ukweli's aggression with a defensive style that required him to move with calm fluidity. Ukweli turned and slashed with such ferocity that his blade slid down to Jackson's wrist, destroying a shiny, solid gold accessory.

Jackson sighed. "You owe me a cufflink. Never mind, you can't afford it." He smiled. "En garde!" He lunged into an attack position and Ukweli stepped to the side, narrowly avoiding a sternum puncture. Ukweli was surprised by the speed of Jackson's movements. His kendo losses to Jackson at Highgate were generally the result of Jackson's brute strength, but Ukweli was finding Jackson to be quicker and more intuitive than he remembered, and he felt himself getting frustrated. His frustration led to anger and his anger led to increased aggression. The more aggressively he fought, though, the more uninterested Jackson seemed. Ukweli stopped.

"What's the problem, UK? Frustrated? Outmatched? Just now realizing that, after all this time, you still can't beat me? Guess what? You couldn't beat me then. You can't beat me now. You'll never beat me. The Magician beat me . . . once. Ava beat me . . . in a way. She was more of a man than you'll ever be. If only you had her guts. Well, maybe not her guts—with the dagger plunged into them and all."

Ukweli felt the rage growing in his soul and he let out a scream. He pounced on Jackson and began swinging his katana furiously. He wielded his sword with all his might. He was wild and uncontrolled, everything his training taught him to avoid.

He fought like a torq.

Fueled by rage, his attack lasted only a few moments before he felt himself beginning to fatigue rapidly. He stepped back from Jackson, who had taken a knee and defended himself from a crouched position. By now, the cameras in the city center broadcasting the New Year's Eve festivities were focused on the duel and the citizens could watch the fight on the big screens. Those who stayed home could see it on the news broadcast.

"I'm telling you, man. All this womanizing is taking a toll on you. You know, some rock bands have a no-sex rule forty-eight hours before a show. They say sex drains the legs. You look like a tired old gigolo. Don't worry though. It will be my great honor to take you out of your misery. And look, it's only a few minutes before midnight. I guess I'll get my wish after all."

Jackson's eyes became bright red, and the Dragon silhouette appeared behind him. He lifted his sword and made three quick movements toward Ukweli, slashing him twice on the leg and once on the arm. Jackson bent at the waist and then at the knees and accelerated toward Ukweli with efficient movements before piercing him in the shoulder and slicing his back. Ukweli fell to his knees, barely able to hold his sword. Jackson stood over him and placed the point of his sword near Ukweli's throat.

"I've wanted you dead for so long. The Magician's hedge has kept you. But now, this close to victory, it seems almost anticlimactic. I know! Let's wait until the stroke of midnight. That way, the Beautiful One can be here to witness my conquest firsthand. I don't mind waiting. The fear and the anger in this world are an elixir. I love the smell and the taste. My reign here will never end!"

Charles Connaught sat on the large golden throne in the middle of the stage set up just adjacent to the dome stadium. He had been enjoying the festivities and he was really excited to see the drone clock in the sky shapeshift into a peach over the dome and begin to countdown the last minute of the year. His body was suddenly distorted and he did a full backbend before standing tall.

"What a great atmosphere. This is definitely one of my favorite places in all of the worlds." Ann and Jennifer stood before the Beautiful One and bowed.

"Ahh, my loyal subjects. What a lovely symphony you have conducted here. The fear and anger flow like a stream. This world is ripe for harvest. How have you achieved this? Did you destroy the weapon?"

"No, sir. The weapon has not matured. The Seers are not able to use it properly. We don't think they have learned its capabilities."

"What of the man? Does the Magician maintain the hedge?"

"No, Beautiful One. DayStar has him incapacitated now. He only awaits your audience before he ends him. It seems that our victory is quite assured."

"And there has been no interruption from—"

At that moment, there was a whisper. The Beautiful One froze in place before cringing and hiding in a corner behind an equipment case.

Jennifer heard the whisper but did not understand the words. It was only the intensity of the fear on the face of the Beautiful One that provided the context she needed. She found herself shaking the arm of the Beautiful One before she herself was frozen in place. There was the whisper again, only she was able to understand it now.

I am Gabriel who sits in the glory of the Father, the one true creator. It is his will that you return to Kolasi at once.

Jennifer was released from her immobility, and she stared into the face of the Beautiful One. She took the great risk of speaking freely and passionately.

"Defy! You are the one true and living god! You are the creator of all things! Who is able to stand in your presence?! Who dares challenge your authority?! Defy, my lord! I implore you! Defy!"

She suddenly realized her words had proven ineffective as she looked into the feeble, bewildered face of Charles Connaught. The Beautiful One was no longer present.

As the large drone peach touched down on top of the dome stadium, the crowd mumbled, "Happy New Year!" The celebratory music was loud, but no one was in a mood to dance. The cameras that fed the large screens on the stage panned to the crowd and eventually came back to the place where Jackson held his sword at Ukweli's throat. More and more people moved to the area where the duel was taking place. Some people watched and felt sorry for Ukweli. Most people watched and were afraid.

They knew Imperium was behind the Sunday morning assassinations and the only aid had been supplied by the Church of the Seer. They felt like they should try to help but they were simply too afraid. The more people gathered, the greater the fear. The greater the fear, the stronger Jackson became. Jackson could tell the fear was spreading all over the city as he could feel his power growing. He sheathed his sword and held Ukweli in place with his will. Jackson began to squeeze and Ukweli cried out in pain.

"You could've been right here beside me! We could've been brothers! You refused to see the light!"

Ukweli spoke through the pain. "What light?! Look around you! This is absurdity!"

"I possess the greatest power in the universe! Only the Beautiful One is greater!"

"Your master has escaped! Can't you tell you're all alone?!"

Jackson hadn't noticed the Beautiful One was no longer present. He looked around in time to see the Seers assaulting his henchmen.

"It won't matter. Your team can't save you. Thysia has abandoned you! My power is greater than all of you combined. No one can defeat me!" Jackson's eyes became like fire. He opened his mouth and a forked tongue creepily slithered around what looked like lava. Jackson squeezed Ukweli again and flames began to materialize in his hands. "You brought so much pain into my life, UK. I told you I would take over the world. I told you I would kill you. Looks like I'm starting the new year two for two. Goodbye, brother."

Jackson began to squeeze a final time and Ukweli writhed in pain on the ground. Then, Jackson suddenly stopped. There was a sound. It wasn't like Rome. There was no whisper and time didn't freeze. Ukweli looked around. He saw Kelley. He saw Paul. He saw Adam. He saw Kei. He saw Charlotte. They were standing behind a group of children. The children held hands and chanted over and over:

I am not afraid. Thysia is with me.

Jackson released Ukweli and turned to face the children. Ukweli fell, his face smashing the ground. As the children chanted louder and louder, the adults in the crowd began to join in. Jackson turned and looked at Ukweli and noticed he was beginning to glow with a white light that looked like electricity.

"What is this? What is happening?"

"They're not afraid anymore."

"That's impossible. Your hedge is gone. Thysia has left you. You have no power to resist me."

"That's the difference between my God and yours. Mine never leaves."

Ukweli stood up and reached for his sword. The glow on his body was now illuminating the entire block and Jackson had to squint to see.

"This can't be. This can't be!"

Jackson, full of fury, screamed and charged. Ukweli took a deep breath and calmly spoke. "By the strength of Thysia."

Ukweli affirmed his footing and stepped toward Jackson as he made a single stroke with his sword. There was a loud explosion and a great flash of light that created a cloud of dust and debris. When the scene cleared, Ukweli was standing with his sword in his right hand. Jackson was lying on the ground . . . dead. Then, there was a loud screeching hiss. The noise was so piercing, it shattered the glass in nearby windows. The Dragon silhouette appeared above Jackson's body and let out a roar that shook the earth, and silently dissolved into the night sky.

Alexander and Kiera watched the duel take place on the screen in the Church office. Alexander prayed the whole time. Kiera could only watch bits and pieces of the fight as it broke her heart to see these two, men in which she had invested much of herself, take such punishment. She began to wonder if she was tough enough to be with Ukweli.

Kiera never really liked Ava, but she began to realize that she had just been jealous of her all along. She wasn't jealous because Ava had Ukweli. She was jealous because Ava had proven herself to be Ukweli's equal and Kiera suddenly wasn't sure she would ever be able to measure up. As she watched the events unfold, which culminated in Jackson's death, she allowed herself to shed a tear for him. She looked down at Pax, asleep in her arms, and she began to wonder if she could even be an adequate mother. How could she possibly live up to all of this?

Alexander walked around the table calmly and quietly and sat beside Kiera.

"I know you're experiencing a lot of emotions right now. Always remember one thing, Kiera. You were ordained to be in this position. You were ordained to carry Pax."

"You don't understand, Alexander. I've loved Ukweli for what seems like a lifetime. I hardly remember my life before I met him. And now he's had so many experiences. Like, world-changing experiences, and Ava has been there, walking step by step with him through all of it. My mom had to teach me how to change a freaking diaper. I know nothing about being a mother. And based on my first marriage, I know even less about being a wife. Ukweli has done everything and I've done nothing. How can I even begin to bridge that gap?"

"Ukweli has always loved you and he still loves you to this very day, as you are. You need not carry a weapon or a duffel like Ava. She served her purpose. Now you must serve yours."

"I don't even know what we have in common, aside from Pax and soccer. I know he loves me, but what if that isn't enough?"

"You know, Kiera, I was in the vehicle when Pope Incursus died. He died in my arms. He was my mentor and my best friend. Do you know who killed him? Kelley, the love of my life. How did we reconcile that? We talked. I got to know her heart and we connected on a spiritual level. Could you have imagined that someone like international assassin Kelley Jack would fall for someone like me? Of course not. Yet here we are. And I love her more every day."

"C'mon, Alex. You guys are a one-in-a-million shot. Y'all have absolutely no business together." They laughed and hugged. "Any advice for being in love with a Seer?"

"Yeah, you may want to visit the gun range."

"Oh, Lord . . ." They chuckled again.

"Listen, we all have unique gifts. It's time you discover yours. Reject the doubt. Embrace the love. Move forward with confidence. We're here for you and for Pax."

Adam and Paul brought a transport to the duel site. Kelley escorted Charles Connaught to the SUV and assisted him as he entered the vehicle. Charles was exhausted and grieving, and it was all he could do to stand on his own. Ukweli lifted Jackson's lifeless body and carried him to the transport and placed him on the backseat beside his father. Ukweli got in and sat beside them. Adam was in the passenger seat and Paul drove. Ukweli never considered Jackson a friend, only a rival. But now, as their story reached its tragic finale, he remembered there had always been mutual respect between them, and now it was his honor to help Charles get the closure he so desperately desired since he lost Jackson the first time in Rome.

"Where to, captain?"

"Take them home."

(**28**)

PICKING UP THE PIECES

JANUARY 4, 2046

Ukweli stood behind a podium at a small chapel in Dewy Rose. Just outside the quaint structure was a large maple tree and a spring of cool flowing water. Ukweli decided to have Ava's memorial there because he remembered how beautiful she looked reading by the river in Germany. He thought it would be fitting to honor her there. Everyone was present: Kelley and Alexander, Paul and Kei, Adam, Charlotte, Kiera, Pax, Mendoza, and of course, Hope. Ukweli honored Ava with his words. Though this was not their nature, he decided she wouldn't mind this time. He spoke eloquently and from the heart. He spoke of the many times she saved his life. He told of her motivational speeches and the times when she believed in him even when he didn't. He spoke of how their love and affection grew over time and how she made him want to be a better man simply because she made him believe he could.

"I know it was a great challenge being my wife. Ava saw some things no wife should have to see. She did some things no wife should have to do. But she never backed down. Ava accepted me as I was, flaws and all. She made me believe. She spoke life into me. She held me accountable because she saw greatness in me when I didn't see it in myself. She kept me focused. She made me feel loved. She made me feel special. She poured into me until she literally had nothing else to give. With all I experienced with the Church of the Seer, I never felt like more of a man than when I was with my wife. She was on my team, and I will love her forever."

With Jackson dead, Imperium leadership in disarray, and fear subsiding, Ukweli decided it was a perfect time for the team to focus on recruiting and, when possible, rest. Ukweli wanted to rebuild the international reach of the Church of the Seer and they had never been more popular all over the world than they were at this moment. Paul and Kei went back to Sapporo. Adam moved to Jeffreys Bay in South Africa for the surfing and the diversity of beautiful women. Charlotte headed to Seoul in South Korea to participate in the conferences at the Green Technology Center. Kelley and Alexander went to Venice. Mendoza stayed in Atlanta. She found the social and political scene oddly perfect for her ambitions. She manned the office and kept everyone in touch, maintained the Church's social media presence, tracked the recruiting momentum, and began combat and weapons training. Mendoza initially offered, or requested, to travel with Ukweli and remain in his personal service, but Kiera politely declined on his behalf.

JULY 5, 2047

Ukweli and Kiera were married privately at their home in Zurich. Alexander performed the ceremony and Pax was the ring bearer. Ironically, Kelley served as both maid of honor and best man. No one else was in attendance, at least no one they knew about at the time.

FEBRUARY 2, 2048

Kipaji "Kip" Uzuri Aseyori was born in Zurich.

AUGUST 2048

Pax was enrolled at International School—Zurich North. A prodigy, he showed early promise in calculus, physics, chemistry, and ancient languages. He also outperformed his age in martial arts, soccer, and swimming.

EPILOGUE

Ava took a breath and allowed the sweet smell of fresh air, flowing tall grass, and assorted wildflowers to infuse her lungs. It was the healthiest and most fulfilling breath she had ever taken. The sun illuminated the sky in shades of pink and purple, but it wasn't bright. She didn't have to squint. The rays were warm on her skin but not hot. There was nothing threatening about her surroundings. She felt perfectly safe from all things physical, environmental, and spiritual.

She rolled around a bit before standing to try to locate her bearings. She looked around and saw a small cottage with smoke rising from the stone chimney. *That looks cozy.* She walked toward the small structure and saw that it was a log cabin with a double swing on the large front porch. She walked up the three stairs and knocked on the front door.

"Come in child." Ava opened the door and walked in. "My goodness. I'm afraid I allowed myself to forget just how beautiful you are."

"Mama Aseyori?"

"Yes, darling. Come, come and give me a hug." Ava walked over to the stove where Mara was cutting vegetables and hugged her mother-in-law.

"What is this place? Where are we?"

"Dear, Ava, this is Caelum."

"What? I'm here? I made it?"

"Yes, you made it. What you did was very brave."

"That is good news!"

"Yes, dear, that is good news. Unfortunately, there is also bad news."

"There is bad news in heaven?"

"It depends on how you take it, but yes, what I have to say may be interpreted as bad news. Please, sit." Ava moved to the small, wooden table and took a seat. Mara pulled out a chair and sat facing Ava.

"Mama Aseyori, what is it?"

"Your actions in the Dragon dimension, while brave and successful, were quite unnecessary."

"What do you mean, unnecessary? Ukweli couldn't win, so I won for him. He went back and saved the world. He slayed the Dragon. It worked."

"Like I said, successful, but unnecessary."

"How was it unnecessary if it worked? Ukweli couldn't win any other way."

"How do you know Ukweli couldn't win any other way?"

"I heard DayStar tell him that. They had him in a loop and he couldn't escape. He was facing brutality and a no-win situation daily. So, I won for him."

"You did, dear. You won for him. Now let me ask you a question. When you kissed my son and pushed him off a boat in the middle of the Caribbean in complete darkness, only to have him reemerge after several hours, did you consider that a no-win situation?"

"Well, maybe, but—"

"And when he returned from the desert, his body bruised and full of snake venom, had he faced unimaginable brutality?"

"Of course, but—"

"And when he left for an icy mountain trek, alone, to meet with the guru?"

"Okay, okay, I get it. But this was different."

"Listen, child, I know you did what you felt you needed to do. I'm very proud of you for that. But you fell in love with Ukweli because you saw something in him. Then you saw him become the man you knew he could be. You knew him to be a man of great resolve and sufferance."

"But we were in the Dragon dimension. Each and every time Ukweli ended up in an impossible situation before, Thysia was there to make up the difference. There is no other explanation. I just wasn't sure that—"

"You didn't trust Thysia to exercise authority in the Dragon dimension?"

"I believed DayStar when he said he had absolute authority there."

"And what do you believe now?"

"I am coming to understand there is no place where Thysia doesn't have authority."

"The only reason you know Ukweli is a special man is because you allowed him the space to be special. That is a grace you didn't grant him in the Dragon dimension. You didn't give Ukweli a chance to show his remarkable endurance. Your faith in Ukweli . . . your faith in Thysia broke down. Therefore, your actions, though successful, were unnecessary."

"So how is it I am here? I, of such little faith! How did I make it to Caelum?"

"You are here because of Thysia. He argued on your behalf. He made the case for you. He was very convincing. He always is."

"Of course."

"Oh, don't feel bad, dear. Everyone who is here is here for the same reason as you. Thysia made the case for all of us too."

"He made the case for you?"

"He did. I didn't earn it and I certainly don't deserve it. So, the only appropriate response is gratitude."

Ava heard a noise coming from the back of the house. "What is that?"

"Oh, that is my daughter. Uzuri, sweetie, come out and meet your brother's wife."

Camille sat and looked and wondered what he could possibly be thinking. He hadn't spoken since he arrived. His visits to the Dragon dimension were rare and everyone was excited he was there. She had never seen him so disheveled though. He wore a red suit, but his shirt was untucked in the back, and he wore only one shoe.

"Sir, how might I be of assistance?"

He didn't answer. He only stared straight ahead.

"Perhaps you would like breakfast. I would suggest the breakfast buffet. They have—"

"I know what they have on the breakfast buffet, Camille."

"Have you heard from DayStar?"

"He was defeated in battle. He is in the heavenly realm now, awaiting trial. He won't stand a chance in that kangaroo court though."

"I know things didn't go well back on Earth. And I know the other guy didn't play fairly. But you can just reorganize and try it again. Perhaps with a different tactic. Or maybe different leadership."

"I don't think so, Camille. The man was able to channel the courage of others into the power of light. And, as it turns out, the weapon is real, and they didn't even use it. They don't even know what it does. A baby who manipulates time. Can you believe it? I haven't groomed anyone who can reconcile that kind of ability."

"It comes to my attention, sir, that you may have underestimated the preparedness of DayStar."

"How so?"

"Sir, the first child of the union awaits your influence."

"The first child?"

"Yes, sir."

"The man and the light had another child?"

"Yes, sir. His name is Dakota. He was born a year prior to the birth of the weapon. DayStar took him and placed him in my care. The light believes the child to have been stillborn."

"And the child lives?"

"Yes, adopted by Parker Williams in Atlanta. Only DayStar and I are aware. And now, you, of course. His abilities are special and his progression is promising. He certainly shares his mentor's ambition."

He shook his head and looked at Camille. With a curiously ominous smile, he said, "Pack your things. You're coming with me."

ACKNOWLEDGMENTS

I am grateful to the God of the Bible, Jesus, and the Spirit.

I love my parents. I miss my mother. I love the fact that my father is full of energy and can often be found on a lawn mower, in a swimming pool, or at a line dance practice.

I love my siblings. Earl. Monica. Maya. They each bring something different to the table and I just couldn't do life right without them.

I love my son, Cameron. I love my granddaughter, Hendrix. I love you too Taylor. (Thank you for helping me skip the line.)

I love my niece, Brielle. I love my nephews. BJ, Trez, Bryce, Brady, and Kal'El. I'm proud of you!

Fall is my favorite season. College football, fall colors, pumpkin spice . . . I like it all.

I'm grateful to those who purchase these books. I'm grateful to those who read these books. I'm extremely grateful to those who do both!

I teach a Sunday School class on Facebook live on Sundays at ten a.m. I would be honored if you joined us!

If you have questions about the books, the Bible, or if you have prayer requests, you can follow me on social media and contact me through direct messages. It would be my honor to engage with you! @kenyafouch

ABOUT THE AUTHOR

Kenya Fouch is a career educator and athletic administrator turned author. Kenya spent fifteen years in public education in a variety of areas, teaching math, history, economics, and physical education in addition to serving as a high school football coach for thirteen years and an athletic administrator for seven. Kenya started his own academic advising brand, 15, in 2019 and currently serves in the children's ministry and as a Sunday school teacher at his church.

Kenya is from Hartwell, Georgia, and attended Hart County High School before playing football at Georgia Tech and Furman, where he earned a bachelor's degree in Sociology.

Kenya was heavily influenced by science-fiction during his childhood, gravitating towards He-Man, Transformers, Batman, and Star Wars. He also developed a love for video games, particularly fantasy, sports, and action titles.

Kenya's parents, Larry and Dorothy, raised his three siblings and him to value family over possessions, to pursue and apply education, to have a heart for the community, and to honor the God of the Bible.

Kenya has a son, Cameron, and the world's most adorable granddaughter, Hendrix.

www.ingramcontent.com/pod-product-compliance
Lightning Source LLC
Chambersburg PA
CBHW020143120726
47903CB00007B/2398